Seven Minutes In Heaven

Kat Fletcher

Copyright © 2015 by Kat Fletcher

All rights reserved.

No part of this book may be reproduced in any form or by any electronic or mechanical means, including information storage and retrieval systems, without written permission from the author, except for the use of brief quotations in a book review.

If you enjoy this book, please visit us online

www.katfletcher.com
Twitter: @kfletcherwrites
Facebook: www.facebook.com/kfletcherwrites

Contents

Prologue	1
Chapter 1	6
Chapter 2	14
Chapter 3	19
Chapter 4	30
Chapter 5	33
Chapter 6	39
Chapter 7	46
Chapter 8	48
Chapter 9	52
Chapter 10	66
Chapter 11	73
Chapter 12	78
Chapter 13	84
Chapter 14	92
Epilogue	108

Prologue

July 1998

Megan was thirteen the year it happened or, as she insisted at the time, almost fourteen. Labor Day weekend, the nights beginning to feel chilly and the first days of high school lurking only a week away. These visits to Cape Cod were part of the rhythm of her year, the vacation home having been in the family since before her mother was born. The sprawling colonial sat across the street from a cottage colony in Dennisport. The beach, visible from the upstairs windows, only a few minutes' walk away.

The adults left her and her cousin Josh alone for the day with advice not to wait up and an overoptimistic suggestion they not have guests over. Josh responded in the predictable manner by immediately inviting the other teens in the neighborhood, whether he knew them or not.

"How old are you anyway?" the boy asked. Megan didn't know him. He was tall and dangled a can of beer just outside of Megan's reach.

She should have known they weren't going to let her in on the beer. Josh was three years older and for the past few years, these summer reunions had been horrible affairs of a surly teen avoiding being stuck with an equally surly preteen. This year, he'd grudgingly allowed her to tag along, but there were still limits. Worse, she knew if she lied about her age that Josh would only correct her, making the embarrassing situation worse. "Almost fourteen," she answered.

The older teens erupted in laughter. "Why is this kid here anyway?"

Josh's explanation wasn't kind. "She's my cousin. Our parents stuck me with her." He turned to her and offered a ten-dollar bill "Go to the store and get us some munchies."

Megan crossed her arms and narrowed her eyes to indicate she was not going to be doing "little kid errands" for him anymore.

"Go," Josh insisted.

She fumed and rolled her eyes, but took the money and headed out the door, across the street, and down the gravel path to the cottage colony's combination office and convenience store. Andi was sitting outside looking bored and gave a silent wave. She was the same age, but Megan's parents didn't approve of the local girl whom they referred to as "the caretaker's daughter." This, of course, only increased her allure to Megan and they'd been meeting at the beach or exploring the neighborhood together for the last week.

"What you up to?" Andi asked, following her into the store.

"My cousin got some beer and they sent me for munchies."

"OK, if I come over?"

"Sure. That'd be cool," Megan answered, relieved she'd have someone to hang out with. When they got back to the beach house, loud music was playing and the rest of the kids were sitting in a circle in the living room. The beer was gone.

"Hey, it's Andi-the-Man-dee," one of the guys said in a disgusted tone.

"What's *it* doing here?" a girl asked, making a face.

"She's my friend. You got your chips, so leave her alone," Megan said, standing up to the older girl.

"If she's your friend, maybe you two should play a round of the game too," the puss-faced girl said smirking.

"Oh fuck, that'll be a laugh," another kicked in, his voice a little slurred.

"Yeah, it'll teach you to bring strays home," Josh said as the others laughed and egged him on. He grabbed the two young girls by their shoulders and started pushing them across the room. Throwing the closet door open, he shoved them in. "Seven minutes in heaven. Have fun!"

As the door shut and a lock clicked behind them, they slumped to the floor, bodies pressed against each other in the tiny dark space, jackets swinging above their heads.

"Sorry, my cousin isn't usually such a jerk." What had gotten into him, she wondered. Just the beer?

Andi shrugged. "I think he's a little drunk. Don't worry, I'm used to people being shitty to me. Most summer people aren't as cool as you."

She was cool? That was welcome news to Megan. She'd been willing to invoke her parents' wrath to hang out with Andi, but always felt a little intimidated by the other girl. She'd more than once wondered if Andi really was her friend or if she was just hanging out because there was nothing better to do.

"Is that what they call you?" Megan asked, horrified at the insult from her cousin. "Andi-the-man-dee? I don't get it. Because of your short hair? That's horrible."

Andi stared at her smirking. "Wow? Really? You don't know?"

Megan shook her head, embarrassed, "No. What am I supposed to know?"

"It's not so much the hair. It's... Well... I kind of, well, it's not kind of. I like girls."

Megan's heart skipped a beat. "Like you're gay? No way!"

"Way!" Andi said, doing her best Wayne's World imitation and sending both of them into giggles. "I got caught kissing another girl in 7th grade. I can't believe it wasn't the first thing someone told you about me. You really didn't know? No wonder you were so nice to me."

Megan looked at Andi again, examining her as closely as she could in the limited light. She'd never met anyone gay before. It was kind of like her eyes were refocusing to bring one of those weird hidden pictures into focus. The short hair, little attention to makeup or anything like that, loose boyish clothes. How had she not noticed before? It didn't matter to her, Andi seemed cool. "I don't care if you're gay. You're one better off than me. I've never kissed anyone," she admitted.

"You're serious?" Andi looked surprised. "Cause you're wicked cute." There was an awkward pause. "Sorry, maybe I shouldn't say that."

"It's OK," Megan smiled. "So we're supposed to kiss in here?"

"That's the game. Spin the bottle and go in with someone. I don't think your cousin wants you to make out with another girl. He thinks you'll be grossed out by being stuck in a closet with the local dyke. Don't worry, we only have like five more minutes left. Unless they forget about us. How much beer did they drink?"

Megan shivered despite how warm the closet was becoming. "We can. If you want. Kiss."

"You really want to kiss?" Andi asked surprised.

"Do you really like girls?"

"Yeah," Andi whispered.

"Then yes, I really want to kiss," Megan said, boldness coming from where she wasn't sure.

Andi lifted her hand and brushed some of the hair away from Megan's face. She felt a flutter in her stomach as they leaned closer. "Are you sure?"

Megan nodded, both entranced and terrified.

Chapter 1

"Welcome to Cape Cod 2014" the billboard in the shape of giant license plate said. *Liar*, Megan thought. This wasn't really Cape, it was still miles to the bridge. She glanced at the clock on the dash. A little after one. She'd stopped for the night at a little chain motel once she'd gotten past the New York City traffic and into Connecticut and slept in late. She could have made the trip from DC to Massachusetts in a single ride, but she needed to pick up the key and didn't want to be knocking on the caretaker's door at midnight.

Yeah welcome to Cape, she thought to herself as the Bourne Bridge came into view. Cape Cod didn't hold a lot of good memories for Megan, at least not recently, and this visit was unlikely to create any new ones. Visit? Was it even fair to call it a visit? Exile would be more accurate. Once over the arching span, the GPS began to bark "Take the third right" at her. The overloaded car was sluggish going around the rotary. Another reminder. Why shouldn't the vehicle be a little rough turning? All her earthly possessions, the physical summation of a life of not quite thirty years, now just a pile of rubble in the back of the small station wagon.

Fuck him anyway, she thought.

She pulled off the highway and headed down the smaller local roads towards the oceanside beaches and the house. Curious about how it had weathered the winter, she decided to drive by quickly before picking up the key. Once the house came into sight, she pulled to the side of the road and ran the window down letting the car fill with the crisp April ocean air. It had only been what? Eight months since she and Michael had last visited for the big Labor Day weekend family reunion; reenacting her childhood, except with more wine and this last year, with more passive aggression.

A for-sale sign caught her eye, advertising one of the cottages across the street from the beach house. They'd been turned into condos a few years ago and sold off. As a child, she'd played with a lot of the kids whose families rented and she wondered what happened to all of them. It had been the same people year after year, and unlike her family and the others who owned the old homes, they weren't well off. She didn't see any of them likely to have a hundred thousand dollars sitting around so they could buy the little cottages they used to rent. A shame. The real tragedy was the wonderful little mixed community she grew up enjoying was gone, but she supposed that was a metaphor for the whole economy.

Stop being dreary, she thought to herself and headed to pick up the key. The address for the property manager wasn't even a mile down the shore road, but didn't seem like an office, more like a small house. Looking more closely, behind the house was a dirty Subaru Forester with a short trailer holding a mower and some other landscaping equipment. Megan figured it had to be the place and parked. She got out and rapped a few times at the door and a dog started to bark inside by way of answering.

The door opened. "Let me guess, you're Sharon's daughter?"

Attractive. Very attractive. The thought sprang into Megan's head the moment she laid eyes on the woman. Not pretty in the sense of conventional beauty, but cute nonetheless in a simple straightforward sort of way. Tall with an athletic, almost boyish, figure, dressed in faded jeans and a plain gray hoodie. A series of captive bead rings led up one of her ears, easily visible through the short sandy blond hair. Her face was somehow familiar. "Yes," Megan answered, distracted by the woman, trying to place who she resembled.

"Come on in and I'll get the key."

A little black and brown Yorkshire Terrier skittered around her knees, all yips and snorts. Megan leaned over to give him a pet. "And who are you furry one?" Megan asked, letting the dog sniff her hand, and ruffling the fur to the animal's delight.

"That's Lola. She's friendly. I guess you figured that out." Megan could hear the amusement in the woman's voice. "A little jumpy, but she won't hurt you. In fact, I'd say she likes you."

Megan stood up and looked around. The door opened into an attractive, but disorganized living room crowded with furniture and bookshelves. It was pretty in its own homey way with a plank wood floor covered by a festive braided rug. A couch sat against one wall opposite a flat screen TV on which a Red Sox game was playing with the sound turned down. On the plain pine coffee table, a laptop perched precariously on top of a stack of books. What little of the pale tan walls not hidden by bookshelves was covered with art. Photos. Paintings. Framed fabric pieces.

She recognized a Hopper print, "Chop Suey." She'd seen the original at the National Gallery when she'd been in college. Two women sitting together at a Chinese restaurant. Giving the room another look, it seemed like most if not all of the paintings and photographs were of women. She felt a nervous flutter in her stomach realizing why the woman seemed familiar.

"Andi-the-Man-dee?!" she blurted out. The minute it left her mouth, she raised her hand, covering her lips in horror. The words hung in the air like an unpleasant odor and the other woman turned around and stared at her. "Oh my God, I'm sorry," Megan gasped.

After a moment of surprise, the tall woman smiled at her and chuckled. "It's OK, I haven't heard anyone call me that since, well, since I left the unhallowed hell of high school."

Megan's thoughts raced. Would Andi recognize her? Megan, of course, could never forget her. "Oh my God, I'm so sorry for the verbal diarrhea. When I saw you at the door, it was driving me a little crazy. I knew I recognized you, but I wasn't sure where from. When I figured it out, the words just came out."

"It's alright. Really," she flashed another cute smile. "It's not like I did much to push back against people calling me that. I was pretty pissed off at the world and think I kind of liked how uncomfortable people were. Anyway, your house is all set. Electricity's on. I turned up the heat and hot water and took the cable out of suspension. There's internet too. Well, you probably know all that."

"Thank you. I know where everything is. My husband and I were just there over Labor Day weekend. I've been coming to Cape every year since I was a girl." She wondered if the prompt would elicit a reaction from Andi.

"Your mom said—about you and your husband—sorry," she shrugged awkwardly. "Here you go," she held the key out.

Megan extended her hand and the woman dropped it into her palm.

"If there's anything you need, just call." She lifted her hand indicating to wait a moment. "Hold on, I have cards somewhere." She wandered over to a shelf and rifled through the books and objects. Megan couldn't help smiling at her slightly scattered manner. Finally, she pulled out a little wooden box and took a business card out. "There, my number and email, either one to get in touch. Never know with these old houses if something's going to break when you open them back up."

Andi Thatcher
Landscaping — Small Repairs
Property Management

Megan took the card and waved it, smiling at the tall woman. "Thanks, I'll give you a ring if I need anything. Again, I'm sorry. If it means anything, back when we were kids? I never called you that."

•••

The key slid into the lock and turned cleanly. It felt odd to be opening up the house alone. Her mother or grandparents or some distant aunt or uncle had always been there when she had arrived. The house wasn't small and as she stepped into the entry, it seemed like the click of her shoes on the hardwood floors echoed against the lonely walls. The air was stale, a vague musty smell competing with the salt breeze from outdoors.

When she saw the closet door in the living room, a rush of memories came back. *Andi was still on Cape. That was* a surprise. Megan imagined her in San Francisco or something like that. She'd seemed so sure of herself.

Leaving her purse on the dining room table, Megan brought her suitcase up the narrow steep stairs and paused at the landing. She looked in through the open door at the first bedroom. Her yellow one-piece was still draped over the foot board of the queen bed. She'd wanted one last swim before they started back for DC, but had never gotten around to packing it before they left.

This had been her room since college, but she had no intention of sleeping in it. Her mother had been, well, somewhat more than merely approving of her relationship with Michael. There had been none of the fussing about unmarried lovers sharing a room, instead her mother had quickly and efficiently moved them in together from the first time he visited during summer break.

She didn't fancy taking her mother's room either, so that left the "kids' rooms." She put her suitcase on one of the twin beds and sat on the other, testing it. This was where she'd slept every vacation until college, it would work for now. It was her house, at least for now, and she supposed she could even swap the furniture around if she wanted more space.

She considered unpacking the rest of the boxes in the back of her Jetta wagon, but those could wait. She went back downstairs and searched through the kitchen cabinets. The little blue packets of Sweet & Chemical and powdered creamer were right where she remembered. The coffee remained elusive. She knew it had to be somewhere and finally checked the freezer. *Score!* She pulled out the container of dark roast, its heft indicating there was plenty left in the can.

After the machine was set up and the caffeinated elixir gurgling into the carafe and filling the room with a pleasant aroma, she plucked out her phone and found her mother on the contact list. She had promised to call when she got in, but dealing with her mother was the last thing she wanted. Megan didn't want to be resentful, but it was hard not to be. A reprieve came from the coffee maker as it sputtered and steamed, letting her know the pot was done. She poured herself a cup, mixed in the sweetener and cream powder, and took a sip. *Note to self, buy real half and half.* Better than nothing, but she was somewhat of a coffee snob and this was simply not up to standard.

Restored by the caffeine rush, she picked up her iPhone to get it over with. One ring, then two, a third. Could she get lucky and only have to leave a message? "Hello Megan," the voice was passionless.

"Hi mom," Megan tried to be cheerful, "I wanted to call and let you know I got in."

"I appreciate that. And that woman got everything turned on?"

"Everything is fine and she gave me her card if anything needs work. And she's not 'that woman,' her name is Andi. She seems very nice."

"Her name is Andrea, I'm not sure why she wouldn't want to use such a pretty name."

The thought was so silly, Megan almost laughed thinking about it. Obviously she was an Andi not an Andrea and Megan couldn't imagine the woman ever wasted time trying to be anything she wasn't. "That's up to her. We all make our own choices mom."

"Well you certainly have," her mother snapped back.

Megan didn't answer. *If I hadn't listened to your sage advice, I wouldn't have married Michael and I wouldn't be in this mess,* she thought to herself. The call was going downhill fast. Maybe the phone could possibly just lose the signal? This was Cape Cod after all. No cell towers in this back yard and barely two bars. No. Her mother would never buy that. She'd call back and start in on her again.

"Megan?" There was an awkward silence. She was pretty sure what her mother was going to bring up and didn't want to deal with another argument.

"Yes mother?"

"Are you sure this is what you want? I'm certain you and Michael could figure something out. You could make an arrangement."

"Mom, it's not going to work out and he's not going to settle for her being his mistress. Her father is a sitting Congressman for Christ's sake. Michael doesn't care about sleeping with her as much as he does about having a powerful politician as a father in law, so unless you're running for office, it's not going to happen. Ever." She hated how bitter her voice sounded, but her mother had a unique ability to get under her skin and antagonize her.

She wished her cup of coffee were a glass of wine; it was going to be a very long irritating conversation.

Chapter 2

As she walked through the crisp morning air, Megan regretted not wearing something more substantial than the sweater-hoodie. It wasn't frigid and the wind was moderate, at least for the beach, but was chilly enough that she could see little clouds of steam when she let out a deep breath and she was planning to be here for a while.

A gull landed on the sand a few feet away and cocked its head at her. Perhaps the bird remembered the tourists in the summer and their bags of chips and discarded bits of sandwich. "Sorry gull, no food for you today," Megan apologized as she put down her bag and pulled the tripod off and set the legs firmly in the sand. Digging through the bag, she took out the camera, mounted the lens, adjusted the controls, and took a quick peek through the viewfinder. She could capture the curve of the land and still include the quaint little cottages just past the beach. *Perfect*, she thought as she sat down and waited for the sun.

"No girl," the voice came from off the beach, somewhere in the maze of cottages, "you can't run free or you'll break that nice lady's camera."

Megan looked back at them, recognizing Lola and her tall owner, and smiling to herself at the coincidence, gave a little wave.

"I thought it was you. Guess you've found yourself a hobby?" Andi said by way of a greeting.

Megan twisted her body in the sand, trying to stand up without looking too awkward. Andi held a hand out and Megan supposed this meant she wasn't going to hold a grudge over their first meeting. What had possessed her to blurt that out? After getting up with Andi's help, she brushed the sand from her jeans, hoping there were no outward signs of the tingly flush that had gone through her body in reaction to Andi's touch.

"The photography? I got the bug back in DC. My soon-to-be-ex bought this high-end camera for me to keep me busy until I went back to school. I figured I should learn how to use the thing and got hooked. Not that that we ever got around to the 'me going to grad school thing.' But, you don't care about that, so why am I sounding like an idiot and babbling," Megan shrugged.

"Don't worry about it," Andi said cheerfully. "Helps to vent. What brings you out this early?"

"I figured I had to do something or I'd go stir crazy in that big house alone, so I thought I'd take some landscapes. I wanted to catch the light at dawn."

"Yup," Andi replied still keeping the bounding dog at bay, "in about ten minutes the whole beach is going to turn gold. Everyone comes for sunset, but it's usually pretty quiet in the mornings. Most days, Lola and I are the only ones here this time of day, at least until the summer. Once the season starts, you get more walkers and the occasional eager beaver tourist shivering in their bathing suits because they want to wring every minute out of their day at the beach."

She pulled back at the dog's collar again and gave Megan a distressed look. "Sorry, Lola's a little excited and I don't want her to knock over your thingie. It looks, well, expensive."

"Oh sure, we can step away," Megan said, feeling silly she hadn't suggested it, and the two women took a few paces back from the rig so Andi could let out the dog's leash. "Yeah, girl, you need to have some space," Megan leaned over and played with the terrier. "Wish I had something for you, but good dogs don't need coffee."

"She's caffeinated by nature, I think," Andi joked. "I said this the other day, but I think she likes you. She's not friendly with everybody."

"She's a nice dog. With a nice owner, I might add." The moment she said it, Megan worried if she was being too flirty, then considered why she should be worried about that in the first place. Oblivious to her mental conflict, the other woman simply smiled back without any hint of acknowledgment.

"I don't want to distract you from your pictures," Andi said kicking gently at the sand with the toe of her boot, "we should get on down the beach. Anyplace you want us to stay away from so you can get a clear picture?"

"You're not distracting me." Was Andi bored with her already? Megan gazed into the other woman's eyes trying and failing to read her mood. *Wow, are those eyes blue.*

"Everything at the house working alright?" Andi asked, looking at Lola or the sand or anything except Megan.

"Everything's great," Megan said, her eyes glancing once again at Andi, examining the curves of her face and the blush red color of her cheeks brought on by the morning chill. The other woman caught her looking and Megan shifted her eyes away quickly. There was a silence between them as they both looked out at the water without speaking, the only sounds being the crashing waves and the occasional yips from the impatient dog.

"Oh shit," Megan blurted out, noticing the sun creeping over the horizon and realizing she had lost track of time. Now that the light was here, she worked the camera efficiently and obsessively, clicking a few exposures, repositioning or changing settings, shooting a few more, barely aware of anything else around her. Anything else other than Andi watching from ten feet away. Megan cast her an occasional smile or glanced at the other woman. Most of the time, Megan chafed at someone being around while she worked, but somehow she was able to shoot free of the nervousness she usually felt when under observation.

After a frenzy of activity, Megan stepped back, figuring she had enough shots. At least for today. She walked over to where Andi and Lola stood, Andi patiently waiting and Lola a little less so. "Sorry, I get kind of obsessive, but I think I got some good pictures. I won't know until I download them to the computer and see them on a bigger screen."

"To be honest, it was amazing to watch," Andi replied, her voice seeming sincere and a little bit awed. "I can barely take a picture with my phone, never mind all those controls and things."

Megan could feel herself blushing. "I'm just someone who knows enough to get herself into trouble and has the gear to do it."

"You keep telling yourself that. Well, I guess I should get going before my girl here loses her mind," the small dog tugging at the leash.

"Oh, sure," Megan nodded, disappointed, "I need to pack everything back up I guess. It was nice to see you again."

"You too," the tall blond woman hesitated, "maybe I could see some of the pictures sometime?"

"Sure!" Megan answered with a smile.

"Great," Andi started off. Megan watched her intently for a few moments and felt her heart skip a beat when a few dozen feet down the beach, Andi looked back quickly and waved.

Chapter 3

Megan glanced at the clock as she loaded the dark grounds into the coffee maker. Too early to be awake, but not as early as she would have liked. She probably still had time to catch Andi on the beach, provided she had at least a little luck. *Need some luck?* she thought to herself. *Good luck with that.* When was the last time she needed luck and it actually came through? She filled two of the thermal cups and added half-and-half and sugar. Back in DC, "coffee regular" was black, but in New England it meant lots of cream and sugar, which was how Megan preferred it. She only hoped that if that was "regular," it would mean it was to Andi's tastes as well or at least acceptable.

Throwing her pink North Face jacket on, she slung the camera bag around her shoulder, grabbed the two cups, and headed out the door. It was only a few hundred feet through the maze of small cottages to get to the beach. She looked around, but it was empty other than a few sandpipers and gulls flittering around the water's edge, looking for their morning meal. She sat down on the short concrete wall that held back the sand from the sparse lawns of the nearby cottages, the cold sending a shiver through her body as heat leached away through her thin jeans.

She sipped her coffee and waited, occasionally snapping a photo if a bird came reasonably close. "Don't suppose you can see her from up there?" she asked a gull gliding on the wind above her. How long had it been? Ten minutes? Fifteen? Andi taking Lola for a walk had the feeling of a routine to Megan, but maybe the previous morning had only been coincidence? She checked her phone for the time. Only five minutes? *Anxious much Megan?* she thought to herself. Given how short a time it had been, the coffee was disappearing quickly. Finally, she saw them walk onto the beach a few hundred yards down, a tall woman and a dog running free at her side.

Megan waved and collecting the coffees, slogged through the sand to meet them.

"Two days in a row. That's a habit. Let me guess, you've been assigned as my new stalker?" Andi joked.

"Don't be ridiculous. I'm stalking Lola, not you," Megan smirked back, "but I did bring an extra coffee. Just in case Lola brought someone." She handed the cup to Andi, enjoying her befuddled reaction. The other woman struck Megan as a pretty unflappable person and she took making a little dent in that armor as a personal victory. "And of course for you girl," she pulled a dog biscuit out of her pocket, "I have something too. If that's OK with puppy-mommy?"

Andi shook her head grinning. "That's fine. So why are you here?" Andi sounded suspicious. Amused, but suspicious.

"I thought I could get some pictures of her on the beach. You two looked like you were having fun yesterday."

"Sure. I don't mind. Lola *is* a ham," Andi said, still giving Megan a somewhat dubious look.

"Great," Megan said, pulling her camera to her face one handed, she turned and took a quick shot of Andi.

"Hey, I'm not a dog!"

Megan gave her a wink. "No you're not," she replied and drank the last sip of coffee. Tucking the mug in her bag, she started shooting pictures as Lola romped down the long sandy shore.

"So what's the real agenda?" Andi asked suspiciously as they walked down the beach following the terrier.

Megan froze for a moment. What was she doing out here hoping to meet Andi? And why had she been so pleased when the woman and her little dog appeared? "There's no real agenda," Megan said, looking at the tall blonde who clearly wasn't quite buying it. "OK, there's a little agenda. Just something I could use some help with. I want to swap some furniture around the house and I need another person to help me move a queen bed into another bedroom."

Andi nodded. Was that the smallest hint of disappointment on her face? No, she was smiling; it must have been Megan's imagination. "You need help with a bed and I was the first one to come to mind?"

"Something like that," she gave Andi a smirk. "I'm sleeping in the room I used when I was a little girl, but I'm getting a little tired of a twin bed, so I want to move a queen size in. I'm going to paint too, but I can do that myself. I hope. But right now, I want to shake things up a little."

"That's simple enough, I guess," Andi replied. "Should be easy."

"Well, you haven't seen the bed. It's pretty heavy. I could switch rooms, but I don't want to be in the same room my soon-to-be-ex and I used to sleep in when we came here on vacation. This is kind of petty, but I don't want to even think about him ever again."

"Well at least you're mad," Andi said casually.

"Mad?"

"You're angry. At your soon-to-be-ex. I can hear it in your voice. It's a good step. It's healthy. I meet too many women watch their husband run off with the secretary or whatever and only blame themselves."

"Are exiled divorcees that common on Cape Cod?"

"Do you really want to know?" Andi said, raising an eyebrow.

"That's what I was afraid of."

"You can talk about it if you want; Lola's a good listener. She won't say anything and neither will I."

Megan couldn't help but laugh at her invocation of the little black and brown pooch. She was rampaging in the surf halfway down the beach and Megan had given up any pretense of shooting pictures of her. "We met at GW. George Washington University. Michael was political and ambitious. A little too ambitious it turns out."

"Too ambitious?"

"He left me for another woman, but not for love or even sex. Her father's a Congressman in a safe seat and Michael can ride that connection all the way to a K-Street partnership."

"So not just an a-hole, but 100% a dick? Sounds like you dodged a bullet to me," Andi didn't even try to hide the disgust in her voice.

"I should have dodged earlier, but it just sort of happened. One minute we were studying together and the next my mom was suggesting wedding locations. *She* loved him. I'm not sure she'll ever forgive me. Enough. What about you?"

"It's me and Lola and that's just fine right now," she said.

Megan tried to process how she felt about Andi being available. She wasn't displeased and thought she was maybe a little too not displeased than she should be. Plus, she'd always thought of her as someone who had it together in the romance department. Out and proud and always with someone. "I'm surprised, you had all those girlfriends."

Andi stopped walking and cocked her head to the side in a bit of surprise and curiosity. "And how would you know that?"

Megan made a face at her. "I do have eyes. My whole life, my family came here every summer for a couple of weeks. After I got my license, my parents would let me drive down most every weekend as long as my grandparents or someone was here to make sure I didn't get into too much trouble. I saw you around the neighborhood. You were always with a girl. I'm sorry if I assumed too much, but I thought they were girlfriends, not just friends." Understatement of the year, Megan thought. She'd tried to find a time to say hello to Andi, but every time she'd seen her at the store or the beach, she and some girl had not only been together, but usually all over each other.

"No. Not friends, but not real girlfriends, only summer lovers. Looking back, I don't think most of them were even gay, just looking to punch their ticket for a lesbian experience." Her voice was sad, but after a few seconds changed to bemused. "I can't say I didn't have a good time and it's a little funny that there are a good number of housewives who're probably thinking of me when they have sex with their husbands."

Megan swallowed hard, wondering if Andi was including her in that tally. Probably not, she concluded, or Andi wouldn't be so up front.

"So do you want to take care of that troublesome bed now?" Andi asked.

"Would sometime this afternoon be OK? I'd like to clean up a little. Strip the beds and get my stuff out of the way. That kind of thing. Unless your fondest desire is to help me with the laundry."

"Don't remind me, I have enough of that at home. I think I'll take a pass. After lunch? Two o'clock?"

•••

Realizing she wasn't actually paying attention to the book, Megan surrendered and laid the Kindle back on the coffee table. She stood up and looked around to see if there was anything she'd missed. The memory of the mummified plate of food from the previous summer made her cringe. She didn't want Andi to think she was a slob, but what had started as a little tidying had turned into a major spring cleaning.

She picked up her phone to check the time. Ten minutes to two. Would Andi be prompt? Early? She guessed right on time, but a moment later was proven wrong by the sound of a car's tires crunching into the white crushed seashell driveway. So Andi was an early girl. Good to know she supposed. She took a deep breath, irritated at her nervousness. It was just moving furniture.

"Hi," Megan said, perhaps a bit too eagerly, as she opened the door. "Come on in."

"Thanks."

"Can I get you something? Coffee? Diet Coke? Water? Or do you just want to get it done?" Did she have to sound so eager?

"I would love a Diet Coke, but let's get the thing moved first. I hate having work hanging over me."

"I managed to get the mattresses into the other room. Those are easy because I can drag them, but I'm having no luck with the bed."

The bed in question was an enormous cherry four-poster with beautifully turned details and thick solid construction. "Let's see," Andi said, grabbing an edge. It took all her strength to budge it even a few inches off the floor, but that hardly mattered as it was too large to fit through a door in one piece anyway. "It should come apart? I think?"

"It should. There's a bracket, but I can't get it to budge. I'm not sure when the family bought the house, but I'll bet it's been here the whole time. Sometime in the '20s? So almost a hundred years?"

"OK, come here and put your foot on it, then lean all your weight on it when I pull."

Megan nodded and half stood on the footboard. Andi tried to get a good grip and backed into her. "Sorry, maybe put your foot here," she said, putting a firm hand on Megan's shoulder and guiding her to the spot she wanted her at. Megan complied, feeling a little more affected by the other woman's touch than she expected.

Andi yanked again at the recalcitrant sideboard and it suddenly popped up, sending her off balance and onto the floor. She sat back, hands out to steady herself, looking confused as to how she'd gotten there.

"Oh my God, are you OK" Megan asked, trying to suppress a giggle.

"So enlighten me again? Why was this *so* important?" Andi managed to keep her face serious for a few seconds before a broad grin came over her face. She picked herself up off the floor. The first joint unfastened, they made quick work of the others and the bed lay in a heap of heavy cherrywood parts.

"Thank you so much for this," Megan said, straining to hold up her end of the thick headboard. "I realize it's a little silly, but that was never my room. *This* is my room. But I did want the bigger bed, which makes it even stupider because the only time I ever slept in this bed was with Michael."

"It's not stupid." Andi's tone was simple and straightforward without the kind of pity or feigned encouragement Megan might have expected. "You get memories associated with a place. That's human nature."

"I don't miss him," Megan burst out. Where had that come from? She couldn't deny it was true, but why bring it up now? Why in front of this woman who was both a stranger and, because of their past, in some weird way an intimate.

"Your husband?"

"Michael, *soon-to-be-ex-husband*. I don't miss him. I'm not sad. I'm kind of relieved."

"Did you love him?"

The question left Megan feeling empty because she knew the answer, but felt like telling the truth would make it real. Nice girls didn't marry people they didn't love.

"You didn't, did you?" Andi asked. Was it kindness in her voice or pity with a side helping of derision?

"No," Megan finally admitted, clearly and simple. "I guess not. I thought we worked well enough together, but looking at it now, it was what you'd call a professional relationship."

"Well, I'm sorry for that. You deserve better," Andi turned her attention back to the task for a moment, then stopped and looked back up at Megan. "I'm also sorry if I overstepped my bounds."

"You didn't at all," Megan said as they shifted the last piece around the corner into her new bedroom, "it's nice to have someone to talk to and you're very easy to talk to."

•••

"Is the can OK?" Megan asked, holding out a Diet Coke. Her hands were sore from disassembling and rebuilding the bed and the cold can, already dripping with condensation, was a pleasant balm.

"Absolutely," Andi replied, popping the can open and taking a large swallow. "Thanks, needed that."

"I probably should have mentioned the bed was like a hundred years old and weighed a ton."

"I didn't think you were going to ask for help to move a cheap piece of pine from the Scandinavian Store. Plus, I've seen the furniture. Don't forget, I come in once every couple of weeks in the winter and take a little tour to make sure there are no broken windows or hobos living large or whatever."

"Does that happen?" Megan squinched her face into a dubious look.

"Not that much," Andi said, flopping onto the couch. "More often teenagers breaking in looking to raid someone's liquor cabinet. It's not exactly big time crime."

Megan couldn't think of anything to say and silence fell between them. It felt odd, like someone should be leaving, except she didn't want her to leave.

"Before I go. Did you get any good pictures of my girl?" Andi asked.

"Your girl?" Megan spurted out.

"Lola? My dog? You took pictures this morning?"

"Oh!" she blushed. "Yeah. Let me get the laptop. I downloaded them this morning when I got back."

Megan grabbed the MacBook off the table and sat down on the couch next to Andi, trying to get close enough that the other woman could see. The screen lit up as it came out of sleep, revealing a photo of Andi, looking a bit haunted and staring at the water.

"That's not Lola," Andi said, her voice trailing off, "but it's amazing. How'd you make me look that good?"

"You always look that good," Megan replied, suddenly aware they were only inches away from each other. Megan had spent almost an hour retouching the picture on the laptop, getting it cropped just right, switching to black and white, and adjusting the mix of light and shade to bring out the other woman's rugged beauty. She was perfect and Megan couldn't have been more pleased with the result.

"Can you email a copy to me? And wait? When did you take it? I don't remember you taking any pictures of me."

"Oh, I managed to get one or two when you weren't looking." She pressed a key to move on, showing Andi the better shots she'd moved into their own collection.

"These are good."

"You don't have to sound quite so surprised" Megan smirked, reveling in the compliment. She'd thought they came out pretty good, particularly the shot of Andi, but still had trouble trusting her own judgment when it came to photography.

Andi stared at her as if she'd just thought of something. "Can you take pictures of houses?"

"Ok. Odd question. I guess so. I used to take a lot of shots downtown in DC. Here," she said, opening a new folder and showing off her work.

"I still own four of the cottages as rentals. I still have some unbooked weeks and getting people into them is all about how they look on the internet. My iPhone pictures are OK, but not on your level. Do you want to make some money?"

"What?" Megan was honestly incredulous. Pay for her to take pictures? Andi must have lost her mind.

"Sorry, for switching to business, but it's kind of a habit. We all sort of feed off of one another here on Cape. Buy local and all that. I didn't mean to imply you needed money or anything. You are a great photographer though and having better pictures of the cottages would help me a lot."

"I'd be glad to take photos for you, but I have no idea what to charge. I can't let you pay me, it's only a hobby."

"Sure you can. Get on the internet and find a fair price. Trust me, I'll make it back raising the rent for some rich asshat from New York."

"Does that mean I'm no longer a rich asshat?" Megan mused.

"It took me a little while to remember you, but we were friends once, at least for a little while. You always treated me like a person. Rich maybe? Asshat, nope."

"I wasn't sure if you recognized me or not," Megan said, dancing around the subject nervously.

Andi gazed across the room at the closet door. *That closet.* "I remember everything."

"Oh," Megan whispered nervously. She chastised herself silently for feeling this way, but the short distance between them on the couch seemed terrifyingly intimate rather than simply comfortable. She was being ludicrous, worrying so much about something that happened sixteen years ago when she was barely a teenager.

Andi turned to her and their eyes locked. Megan froze, half afraid and half wishing that something might happen. Andi's face was mere foot and a half away. However, she didn't move towards her, just smiled jovially. "You tried kissing a girl. So did every other thirteen year old. Don't worry, I know you're straight. And is there any more Diet Coke?"

Chapter 4

Megan put the glass of fizzy water on the nightstand and plunked herself on the bed. Opening her laptop, she typed "Real Estate Photography" into the search engine and scrolled through the results. The techniques seemed to be pretty much what she'd figured. She clicked on a site for "hideous real estate photos" and got immersed, laughing until tears streamed down her face at the insanity that any of these could actually have been used in a listing. Feeling mischievous, she padded downstairs and looked through her bag. There it was. Andi's card and yes, there was an email address. She ran back upstairs and downloaded a few of the worst photos from the site and attached them to an email. "I have done a few real estate shoots before, here are some examples," then sent the message to Andi.

There were a few other new e-mails. Her mother. She didn't even open that one. Why spoil what had been a nice day. Something from Michael's attorney about papers to sign. She wondered if Andi had a printer. She must. If not, the library. She looked at the figures. At least he was being generous, offering two thirds of the house sale and a year's support in return for going quietly. There was still quite a mortgage, but after it was paid off, her share, would be enough to live on for a few years or pay for grad school.

Another email from whom? The address wasn't familiar esteele@bmail.org? Elissa Steele? Her roommate from college? They'd done the usual perfunctory swapping of Christmas cards, but despite both living in the DC burbs, they hadn't seen each other since graduation. Elissa had hated Michael from the start. She said he was a little too slick, describing him bluntly as "perfect on paper, a piece of shit in real life." Still, she wouldn't be the type to send an "I Told You So" post, though Megan wouldn't blame her if she had. *OK,* she clicked, *here goes.*

> I heard through the grapevine that you and Michael split. I won't pretend to have liked him, but I'm sorry it didn't work out and that I didn't put my feelings aside and be a better friend to you. I hope you're doing OK? I'm still working downtown at the Union offices, if you want to get together for lunch or we could meet after work for a drink.
>
> Elissa

Megan dashed off a reply.

> I think I should apologize. You were right about Michael, he's a complete ass. I'm actually doing well, strangely enough. I'm madder at myself than anything. I'm slowly coming to accept we never loved each other. For my part, my mother kept at me to stay with him and I felt like I was on this amusement park ride only instead of going down a big hill, I went down the aisle. I'm afraid lunch would be impractical, unless you're up for a 400-mile drive. I don't think DC was good for me and I wanted to go home. Mother had other ideas and stashed me in the summerhouse on Cape Cod. I think she's still holding out hope that Michael and I will have some kind of reconciliation, but that's not going to happen.
>
> Cape Cod is empty this time of year, but I think I made a friend.

Her fingers sat idle on the laptop keys as she thought about Andi. She was one of the few people of the same age that Megan had met since moving, but was she a friend? Not a friend yet? Just her mom's employee? There had been the thing when they were teenagers and Megan was uncomfortably aware of those awkward moments of attraction in the past few days. Was she more than a friend? Could she be? Megan had married a man. She was straight. But if she was straight, why had it stung so much when Andi had said so?

> I think I made a friend. Maybe more than a friend. I'm not sure yet. It's too soon and too complicated, but I think I feel more when we're together than I ever did with Michael.
>
> Thank you for reaching out,
>
> Megan

Chapter 5

"I think I have enough shots," Megan said. Andi had retreated into a corner, purportedly trying to stay out of her way while she shot the photos, but Megan had sneaked a few glances. Usually people babysitting a contractor would check their phones or look bored around the room, but there was none of that. Each time, she'd seen Andi's eyes locked on her. And each brief glance had sent a pleasant flutter through Megan's tummy.

Megan turned to her. "That angle should show most of the room. Want to see?"

"Sure," Andi said.

Megan stood close, almost touching. "You press these buttons to go backwards and forwards through the pictures.

"Doesn't look like a cave anymore," Andi noted dryly. Megan laughed, bringing a matching smile to Andi's face.

"Before we go to the next one, do you want to get some food? Andi asked as Megan packed her things back into the camera bag and lowered the tripod. "There's a little place we can grab something. Unless you just want to get it all over with. That's OK too. I don't know if you have something else to do?"

"I'd love to go to lunch with you," Megan replied, flashing a smile at the other woman.

"Oh, good. Let me get that," Andi said nervously, picking up the camera bag off the plank wood floor of the little cottage.

•••

"Hey Lola," Megan greeted the well-behaved ball of fur curled up outside the door. She sprang to life, circling Megan's legs while Andi locked up.

"In the car," Andi said, opening a door, and Lola obediently hopped into the back seat of the Subaru.

"For lunch, let's see what Mindy has on," Andi suggested pulling onto the road.

"Where's Mindy's?"

"Mindy's a person, not a place. More a force of nature than a person if you want to be honest about it. You'll like her."

"OK," Megan replied, intrigued by her not-quite-an-answer.

They drove for about five minutes before Andi pulled the Forester into the empty gravel parking lot of The Clam Basket. The little restaurant was one of those tourist joints serving fried seafood and soft serve that you could find pretty much anywhere on the New England coast, but this had been theirs. Megan remembered countless lunches with squishy belly clams and crisp hot French fries as well as evening bike rides down the shore road, racing through the near dark to get there for an ice cream cone before they closed.

"Only one problem here Andi, the place is closed for the season," Megan said pointing at the sign and boarded up windows.

"Oh ye of little faith," Andi replied, clearly enjoying her little secret.

The two got out and Andi led her to the back entrance of the little place, leaving Lola peeking out of the lowered back window of the wagon. Cardboard boxes were stacked up on the landing and light came out of a door next to an enormous kitchen fan.

"Mindy?" Andi called out, opening the door and ushering Megan in. An industrial dishwasher was against one wall, two huge sinks, and an ice machine added to the crowding. Plastic trays sat on a food service table, stacked almost all the way to the ceiling. The most amazing aroma of something rich and spicy filled the entire place. A definite contrast to the "fried" smell Megan associated with clam shacks.

A short somewhat round woman, around 50 years old, turned around and words began to stream out her mouth in a rush. "Come on in! Andi! You here for lunch? Is this the girl you've been talking about? Hi, I'm Mindy, make yourself at home. You looking for some lunch? I have a big pot of Portuguese soup on or I have some deli meat and I could make you a sandwich or I think there's some hamburger in the freezer if you don't mind eating them on sliced bread."

Megan marveled at her ability to say so much without taking a breath. She caught Andi looking at her, apparently waiting for a reaction. "The girl you've been talking about?" she whispered and gave her an elbow in the side. As the two smirked like naughty children trying to not break into laughter, Mindy led them through the kitchen to the front dining room. While the lights were on, the room still seemed dark and strange with the large plate glass windows boarded against the fall and winter storms, and chairs stacked on the tables.

Mindy shot back out of the room as fast as she'd led them in, leaving Megan and Andi alone.

Andi took a chair off a table and held it out for Megan. "This is one of the businesses I keep an eye on in the off season. Our parents knew each other and we both took over when they retired. She got back last week and has been getting the place ready to open."

Megan sat down as Mindy reappeared, wiping the table quickly and plopping a large Styrofoam bowl filled with a thick soup in front of each of them.

"Portuguese soup!" she exclaimed and sat down.

"Thank you," Megan said, glad to finally get a word in. She stirred the soup, hearty with some kind of greens, beans, potato, and slices of bright red sausage. She lifted a spoonful hesitantly to her mouth, then took a small taste. It was heaven in a bowl, spicy and rich. "This is incredible."

"First time you've had it?" Andi asked, her voice incredulous.

"Yes."

"Everyone knows kale soup," Mindy added, "but I guess most tourists just get chowder. And they want it goopy which I am not going to do no matter how many of them whine."

Andi smirked. "Well, she's not a tourist anymore, so about time she got around to trying it and yours is the best."

"My soup is OK," Mindy said, smiling at the complement even as she deflected it. "Ok for someone half Portuguese. My mother's was better."

Megan couldn't stop eating and in only a few minutes was scraping her plastic spoon trying to get at the last few drops. "More?" Mindy prompted.

"Would it be terrible if I said yes?" Megan asked.

"Not a bit!" Mindy said and whisked the bowl away, returning a moment later. "You two enjoy. I need to get back to unpacking."

Andi grabbed two Diet Cokes while Megan devoured the second bowl, opening each and putting them down on the table.

"Thanks," Megan said.

"No problem."

Trying not be too obvious, Megan studied Andi between spoonfuls. Her blue eyes, the way her hair kind of tangled a little. Her lips, beautiful even without any color. The graceful curve of her neck. The confident even cocky way she sat and held herself. Her body. She seemed thin, but Megan had noticed how fit she was when they were moving furniture. The hint of breasts under her shirt. Were they that small or did she try to make them less obvious? Mere attraction was slowly replaced by a warm flush of desire spreading through her nether regions. It was not exactly unwelcome, but this wasn't the time and Megan took a long drink of her soda and tried to focus on the soup.

"You never answered my letters." Andi said, her voice sounding both pained and serious.

"What?" Megan held the spoon halfway to her mouth. "Letters?"

"When we were kids. After your cousin shoved us in the closet and we... You left two days later and we never got to talk again. I snuck into my dad's office and got your address. I wrote you two letters."

"I never got any letters," Megan replied, lowering her spoon back to the unfinished bowl. "You wrote to me?" She could feel her heart beating as she remember those few stolen kisses. They had meant enough to Andi that she wrote her? Megan couldn't decide if she was relieved she wasn't the only one who'd felt that way or heartbroken that it hadn't come to anything.

"Seriously?" Andi implored. "You never got them?"

"Really, never. I would remember," Megan said, putting her hand on top of Andi's. "I absolutely would have written you back."

"Now I'm sorry I was so pissed at you. Those girls you mentioned the other day?" Andi's voice was a little sheepish. "I may possibly have been playing it up a bit to get back at you. If I saw you around," Andi ran her hand through her hair. "Possibly."

Megan felt her chest tighten. "I never understood why you seemed like you didn't want to see me. Maybe you got the wrong address?" Megan was certain it had been the right address and equally certain of exactly where those letters went, but she wasn't going to drag Andi into her family drama. "I wish I had gotten them," she added, thinking to herself that it sounded so insufficient.

Chapter 6

Megan stormed about the house, working herself up for a phone call. It had been a few hours since Andi had dropped her off and she'd done nothing but let herself get more and more angry. She poured another tumbler of wine. Wine from a box. Another thing for her mother to be appalled by. *Yeah, mom, what about your daughter having a crush on another woman?*

She picked up her phone off the table, put it down again, and went into the kitchen and washed the already empty glass. She dried and put it away and went back and stood staring at the phone and tapping her feet on the floor. Angry.

All because of her mother. The same mother who'd picked at her week after week, phone call after phone call, email after email. "Oh, Michael is such a catch." "Michael's going places." "Michael's so handsome." She'd just gone along. She had nothing particular against Michael and assumed this friendly acceptance was how a relationship was. They'd been happy enough. Functions in DC. Art museums. Sunday mornings with the Post in their townhouse.

She dialed. It rang once before her mother picked up.

"Hello Megan."

"Mother."

"How are you? Have you heard from Michael?"

The woman really was impossible. "I've heard from his attorneys and I've sent them back the papers. We are getting divorced. There's not going to be any last minute change in that."

"Well you don't have to bite my head off," her mother said, her voice defensive.

"Tell me about the letters," Megan demanded, tired of the verbal jousting.

"What letters?"

"Tell me about the letters you threw away when I was a kid. Was it only Andi's? Or were there other friendships you broke up? How much did you manipulate things?"

"The lesbian?" her mother's voice dripped with disdain. "You didn't need to read anything from her. Obviously I looked out for your best interests."

"How could you do that? She was my friend. When I didn't answer she thought I was a complete bitch. What right did you have?"

"I will not be spoken to in that manner Megan, get yourself under control," her mother's voice was not even strained. It was ever the same measured monotone of self-importance.

"You *will* be spoken to in that way. How many other friendships did you destroy?"

There was a moment of silence. "Megan, call me when you can have a civil conversation" and the call went dead.

"You bitch!" Megan shouted at the empty room, raising her arm to throw the phone and thinking better of it, she dialed again.

●●●

Megan got out of the car, the door shutting with a loud clunk as she slammed it with more force than she intended. She was so angry. Angry at herself. Angry at her mother. Angry at Michael. Angry at the universe.

She leaned back against the car for a moment, closing her eyes as the cool metal of the door penetrated her clothes. Counting her breaths, she tried to center herself a little before knocking at the door, but before she could reach "ten" she felt two paws against her thigh as Lola leaned up against her.

"Girl," Andi called the dog back. Megan opened her eyes. Andi was standing in the open doorway, looking at her, concern written on her face.

Megan's breath caught for a moment and then she smiled, relief breaking through her body as she walked to the little cottage. "Thank you for letting me come over," she said quietly as she passed through the door.

"Are you OK?"

"Yes. No. Not really," Megan shook her head, standing arms crossed in the middle of Andi's living room.

"Sit down, let me get you something."

Megan sat on the couch. Another Sox game on the television. She noticed mindlessly they were up by two.

Andi sat down next to her, handing a glass of amber liquid. The two women were not quite touching, but close enough to make Megan's body tingle. "It's bourbon. With how you look, I think booze beats tea and sympathy."

"Do I really look that bad?" Megan asked, feeling her eyes begin to moisten, betraying her.

"Don't ask. Don't tell," Andi quipped.

Taking a tentative sniff, Megan sipped. The flavor was fine, but she was more used to wine and the very occasional beer. Her body shuddered obviously as whiskey went down, embarrassing her. Despite the burn going down, it left a pleasant warmth in her stomach that promised to go to her head quickly. "Thanks, this is perfect."

They sat in silence, Andi at times seeming like she was going to speak, but remaining silent, waiting for the other woman to explain.

"It was my mother."

"Sorry?" Andi asked, not understanding.

"My mother threw away your letters. She's been running my life since I was a kid." Megan stared blankly at the opposite wall.

"It happened a long time ago," Andi said, trying to comfort her. "It doesn't matter."

"You should have heard her when I called her this afternoon. She didn't even remember. When I reminded her, all she could say was 'Oh, the lesbian.' What a bitch."

All Megan could think was what her life might have been if she'd gotten the letters, if her mother had minded her own business and let her live. She'd held onto the memory of those kisses in the closet all winter. "I couldn't wait for summer to see you again. My dad was busy at work and I kept nagging him about how much I wanted to go to the Cape on Memorial Day weekend. He stayed half the night that Friday so he could take the rest of the weekend off and we drove up Saturday morning."

That was the weekend of the blonde. Long flowing perfect golden hair and curves that at fourteen Megan hadn't grown into. Almost the minute her family had arrived at the Cape, Megan made an excuse to walk down to the store to see Andi, but she'd been outside with the other girl. Kissing her. Deeply. On the lips. In public. Megan had abandoned the pretense of buying a bag of chips and walked home, fighting back tears.

I'm a lesbian.

It just popped into Megan's head. Not straight. Not even bisexual. Despite her teenage mooning over Andi, she'd never considered it before. Sex with Michael had been pleasurable, if perfunctory. She had simply assumed that was how it was. Now the reality of it swept over her like the tide on the nearby beach. Her feelings for Andi weren't a crush. Not then or now. The odd sudden bursts of desire that had unexpectedly drifted through her body over the last week were no accident. She wanted Andi. Desired her in a way she'd never felt about Michael. She hoped desperately Andi felt the same way about her, but even if a relationship between them wasn't in the cards, Megan was certain that whomever "the one" turned out to be would be a woman.

"Well fuck me," Megan whispered.

"What?"

"Nothing. I realized something." Megan looked up, feeling suddenly nervous around the other woman. She needed some time to let her revelation settle in her mind before she talked about it with anyone, even Andi. "I just figured out how much my mother has managed to mess me up."

"I'm sure she never meant to," Andi offered.

"I'm sure she didn't care what she did, as long as she got what she wanted. Like I was a project for her, not a person." Megan drained the glass, swallowing hard as the harsh liquor hit her stomach. "Is there more of this?"

Andi had barely touched hers, but got up and brought the bottle, still half full, and poured her another inch. "I'm sorry I brought up the whole thing. Maybe I should have left it alone, but I always just wondered why you never said anything."

"No," Megan said, fidgeting with the glass, "it was good you told me. I knew she was pushy, but I never understood she could be outright deceitful. Isn't that a crime? Stealing mail?"

"I don't know. Seems like it ought to be, but probably it's OK if your parents are the ones who take it. It's in the past, best to let it go."

"Now, I wonder," Megan was babbling now. "There was this girl I was friends with in school, Kate. My mother never liked her. One day in tenth grade, she just stopped talking to me. I couldn't figure out why. I thought I must have done something, but or she decided I wasn't cool enough. Now I'm wondering if it was that something my mom did?"

"Was Kate? You know. Gay?" Andi asked.

Megan laughed, a slight hysteria creeping in. "No, quite the opposite. Completely boy crazy. I think we were friends because I never dated and she didn't have to worry about competition. I still have no idea why my mother didn't like her, but she didn't."

Andi nodded, letting Megan get it out of her system.

"I'm sorry for barging in," Megan said. "I just didn't know who else to call. You're about the only person I've met since moving here."

"That's OK. I feel like we're friends," Andi said, her voice rising as if it might have been a question. "I guess I'm also a part of this as well. At least now I know why you never wrote."

Megan held her glass out again, but Andi raised her eyebrows dubiously. "Please?" Megan pled.

Shaking her head, but a slight grin on her face, Andi poured a splash. "You're not driving home tonight."

"What?" Megan asked. Was Andi asking her to sleep with her? She definitely liked Andi as more than just a friend; did that mean her feelings were reciprocated? Megan didn't think she was ready for that. Was Andi the type to assume she'd just go to bed with her? That didn't seem right either.

Andi laughed, "You look like a deer in the headlights. There's a second bedroom up in the loft. You were in no shape to drive when you got here, never mind after..." she motioned at the bottle on the coffee table. We can stay up and talk all you want, but I have a couple of early morning appointments. You can sleep in and let yourself out or if you don't mind getting up early, you can have breakfast with me.

Chapter 7

Megan's head still hurt, despite the two ibuprofen she'd taken. Before driving home, she and Andi shared a quick breakfast and some very strong, very welcome coffee, but nothing but time was going to solve her hangover. Vowing never to drink again, she pulled out her computer and discovered a new email from Elissa.

> Thanks for writing back. Cape Cod? That's a change. If you want to get back to the city, I'm in Adams Morgan now. It's tiny, but I could pull out the couch for you until you got back on your feet.
>
> Unless of course, that new guy who might be more than a friend works out. :-)
>
> Elissa

Megan peered at the screen, thinking for a moment before a broad smile covered her mouth and she started a reply.

> No, definitely not back to DC. If I don't stay here on Cape, I might apply to grad school in Boston or U-Mass. I loved GW, but if I hadn't met Michael, I don't think I'd have stayed in DC after graduation. It wasn't a great fit for me. Too competitive. Too career oriented. For now, I think I'm just going to enjoy a summer at the beach. Afterwards, I'll figure out the rest.

> There's something else. The jury is still out on that person I met or how they feel about me. I'm absolutely past crush and into something else. Just every time we're together I feel great. I remember you trying to tell me there was something I should have been feeling about Michael and wasn't? I get it now. I know it's quick, but we knew each other for a little while back when I was a teenager. You should know one thing though. I kind of shocked myself, but I kind of figured out why I didn't have that thing going on with Michael. I hope it won't be too weird for you, but this person? She's sort of not a guy.
>
> Meg

She pressed send and it barely took a minute for the response to come.

> Weird that you are falling for a girl? That's silly. The woman I share an office with had a baby with her partner. Would it be rude to say I'm not even surprised? Good on you.
>
> I can't wait to meet her. Maybe I could come and visit sometime? Not now. In a couple of months when I can lay on the beach?
>
> Elissa

Chapter 8

When the phone buzzed, relief flooded Megan's body. It had been two days since she'd spent the night at Andi's and she'd spent them worrying about why she hadn't called. She'd tried to tell herself that the other woman had a business and was just busy, but hadn't been able to shake the worry that she'd overstepped her bounds by calling in a panic or worse, the adolescent fear that the other woman wasn't calling because she didn't "like her that way."

"Hey you," Megan picked up.

"Hello yourself. I hope I'm not disturbing you?"

"Never. I mean, what else would I have to do? That didn't sound very good did it?"

Andi laughed on the other end of the line, "that's OK."

"So to what do I owe the pleasure of your call?" Megan said, trying to thread the needle between friendly and flirtatious.

"I was wondering if you'd like to get lunch with me, either today or tomorrow."

"Mindy's?"

"No, I was thinking someplace actually open. Just sandwiches? Somewhere to chat?"

"Well, I'm free today. Do you want to pick me up or should I meet you?"

"Either one."

"How about I meet you? Where and when?"

●●●

Megan parked on the street, a few doors down from the cafe. Andi definitely had a talent for rooting out the obscure places. How was it possible that she'd walked through this part of town dozens of times over the years and never seen the little sign proclaiming "Port Cafe" or any other indication of the little restaurant. It certainly wasn't a new addition, the aging cardboard poster in the window promising "broasted chicken" was probably there when the Pilgrims landed; she'd just never noticed it.

A bell fastened with wire to the inside of the door gently rang as she went in. The interior was old school diner. A few younger guys were sitting at a lunch counter lined by round stools. Against the front window, there was a row of old fashioned booths, mottled red vinyl coverings and stainless steel frames that probably went back to the 50s. Andi was smiling at her from the last one and gave a little wave, sending a tiny electric buzz up Megan's spine.

"Hello there," Megan slid into the booth.

"Hope you didn't have any trouble finding the place?" *Damn, did Andi have to go to small talk so quickly?* Megan was hoping for something more intimate.

"Nope, never knew it was here, but once I was looking, there it was. It's amazing. I feel like I stepped into a time machine or something."

"I think there's a little bit of magic involved. The tourists never seem to find the place or if they do, they don't eat here. It's mostly the locals."

They pulled menus from the metal frame that also held the salt, pepper, and sugar packets. "Anything particularly good?"

"The meatloaf, but I'd skip the gravy and have them make you a sandwich out of it."

"Sounds good."

Seeing them put the menus down, the waitress came out from behind the counter and took their orders, two meatloaf sandwiches, a large French fry to split, and two chocolate frappes.

"I hope you don't mind," Andi started sounding a little nervous, "but I have been sneaking around a little bit on your behalf."

"Oh?" Megan asked, conspiratorially. "Do tell?"

"Well, there's this woman Sam. She's my ex-girlfriend's ex-girlfriend."

Megan didn't want to think of Andi having any ex-girlfriends, but being technically still married, she didn't think she had a lot of ground to stand on there. Not that she and Andi were anything. Well, maybe showing up and getting drunk on her couch had moved them from acquaintances to friends.

Andi seemed to have picked up her worries. "Anyway, that part isn't important. All in the past. Anyway, here's the important part. You see she owns a gallery in Provincetown. Local artists. Everything from jewelry to paintings. Very eclectic. Very woman centered. You know the picture you took of me on the beach? She thought it was good, so I talked about the landscapes you did and she wants to meet you and look at some of your photos."

Megan leaned back in the booth, pressing into the vinyl, mouth open, utterly astonished.

"You know. For her gallery. Unless you don't want to. That's OK. I thought it might be a way for you to make a little money."

"Sorry!" Megan said a bit bewildered. "I mean. That would be great, but she's probably only being nice."

"I don't think so. She's a great person, but when it comes to her shop? Business? Then she's, well, kind of psycho to be honest. I have her card and I can give you directions. I don't know if you get up to Provincetown very often. The traffic is crazy in the summer, but this time of year it's not even an hour."

"How about you come with me?" Megan said, trying to flash Andi her best smile.

"I guess I could get away for an afternoon. Saturday?"

"It's a date," Megan said. To her delight Andi seemed to pick up on the tone because a questioning look broke out on her face along with a very slight blush in her cheeks. "And I'll be buying you dinner, so figure out where we're going. Someplace nice please."

"You don't have to do that," Andi said, shyly running her hand through her hair.

"You know, for all those girls you tormented me with, you're not very good at this." Did she just say that? Megan wasn't sure who was running her mouth. It certainly wasn't under her control. She only hoped whoever had taken charge kept right on going because she was loving every minute. She felt bold and excited in a way she hadn't in as long as she could remember.

Andi's jaw dropped, apparently equally surprised. "I'm sorry? Are you?"

"Asking you out on a date? Yes. Not just because of the gallery either." Suddenly her nerve ran out and the confidence dropped out of her tone. "Unless you don't want to?"

"No. I mean yes. Yes, I would like to spend the day in P-Town with you. I'd like to go out with you. That would be great."

Chapter 9

It was still just a little too early to pick up Andi. Megan sat in her living room, paging through Andi's Facebook timeline to kill time. They'd added each other as friends a few days ago and Megan had also taken the large and very pleasurable step of changing her relationship status from married to single and sending a screenshot to her mother in a fit of pique. She giggled to herself at the thought. Of course, her mother hadn't replied. Megan wondered if Michael would even notice. She suspected the only social network he cared about was LinkedIn.

Wanting to look perfect, Megan ran upstairs one last time and nervously checked herself in the mirror. It was ridiculous. Since their lunch at the diner, she'd been meeting Andi every morning on the beach and it had only been a few hours since they'd seen each other. It didn't matter though. Part of the ritual of getting ready for a date. Satisfied, she stepped out into the hall, stopped, and turned around. She had to pee. Again. More nerves. Back into the bathroom. Finally feeling ready, she put on her jacket and grabbing the camera bag, went out to her car.

As the tires crunched over the gravel driveway, Lola ran out to greet her, running in excited circles next to the car door. "OK girl" Megan was still petting her when the door opened and Andi stepped out. A ripple of desire went through Megan's body as her eyes took the other woman in. She thought Andi's everyday clothes were cute, but nothing had prepared her for this. Andi strode out confident as ever in a pair of fashionable ankle length boots, dark blue jeans that clung to her lithe body, and a button down western shirt just tight enough to confirm that, yes, as Megan had suspected, Andi had a quite pleasant body when she wasn't dressed for landscaping.

"You're beautiful," Megan blurted out.

"Don't sound too shocked," Andi smirked back. "You look beautiful too. That doesn't count though, because you always do."

They hesitated a moment and Megan stepped forward and took Andi's hand, intertwining their fingers. It seemed like forever until Andi leaned towards her and gave her a tentative kiss on the cheek. Despite its disappointingly innocent quality, the touch of her lips set Megan's skin tingling. Innocent was probably best anyway. Anything more would have been too distracting. She was still nervous, even if the gallery appointment had taken second place in her mind to going out with Andi.

•••

There were barely buds on the trees, much less leaves, but Cape was waking up. As she drove down Route 6, Megan noticed for every business still marked closed for the season, one was already open or at least announcing its imminent return.

"It's kind of pretty," Megan mused.

"What?"

"The Cape before summer. It has a sparse sort of beauty. I think that's why I've been taking so many landscape shots. It's not like the usual sun and fun beach thing. It's more primal."

"Wait until you see a good storm hitting in the middle of winter," Andi replied.

"It'll be an excuse to buy the waterproof lens they just released!"

•••

"Stop!" Andi exclaimed as Megan started to pull into a pay lot in the center of town. It was still two hours until Megan's appointment when they arrived in Provincetown, with its large Victorian buildings, tiny alleys between them, and little shops in every nook and cranny like butter on an English muffin. "It's early season, we can find a spot!"

Megan sighed and pulled back onto the road, driving as Andi rattled off terse instructions to turn this or that way, her eyes darting back and forth like some kind of starving animal in search of prey until she finally found a coveted parking space. "There! Quick."

"You're funny. I could have paid the five bucks in the center of town," Megan teased, easing the car into the open spot.

"But now you don't need to," Andi smirked, obviously proud of herself.

They walked up Commercial Street, looking in various small shops and galleries. Businesses were open and the warmth of the day had brought more than a smattering of tourists, even if the center of town was still quiet compared to the crowds of high summer. As a straight couple with a little boy in tow passed by, Megan noticed them giving Andi and her the once over twice. Amused by their scrutiny, Megan reached for Andi's hand. The other woman peered down. Was the look on Andi's face pleased or skeptical? She didn't let go though and Megan pressed her body a bit closer.

As their hips touched, Andi squeezed her hand. "You're sure about this?"

"Holding your hand?" Megan laughed. "Do you think I'm worried if they think I'm gay? People will think we're a couple whether we do or not."

"Sorry," Andi replied, "you've gone from straight and married to walking in P-Town holding a girl's hand awful fast. You don't have to do that to impress me or something."

Megan stopped and cocked her head up at Andi, giving her a look of impatience. "I'm quite aware of that thank you." Maybe there was a bit of intoxication of the sudden freedom after feeling constrained for so long, but whatever the reasons for her boldness, Megan was dead certain she wasn't going to regret courting the beautiful woman at her side.

"Ok," Andi said, throwing a hand up in surrender, "I'm just trying to look out for you."

When she caught sight of their first drag queen of the day, Megan dropped Andi's hand and hastily pulled her camera out of the bag. She managed to squeeze off a few shots of the six-foot pink blur, dressed in a sparkly mini-dress, and riding a matching skateboard.

She'd always been a little nervous about taking photos of people back in DC, never certain someone wouldn't serve her with a subpoena for violating their privacy. In Provincetown, it seemed perfectly natural to snap pictures in the little town center. People came to be seen. The same sex couples, gleefully expressing their affection openly for each other. The entertainers, busking in front of the town hall. The occasional straight couple, clinging to each other in desperate displays of public affection, lest someone think them part of the local flora and fauna. It was as if the entire town center was part of some grand public performance.

"Oh come on, we have got to go in here," Megan announced, pointing to the window in which a mannequin sat, dressed in a black leather outfit with a flogger on its lap.

"Oh God," Andi groaned, letting herself be pulled into the shop.

"Hello ladies," the clerk greeted them from behind the counter. "If there's anything I can help you with, please let me know."

"Thanks, we're good." He was a younger guy and Megan was mortified at the idea of someone who probably wasn't old enough to drink helping them pick out sex toys. The interior displays were actually quite tasteful, but Megan was taking delight in examining each and everything item with excruciating attention. "Well this looks like fun?" Megan held a pink silicone vibe out to Andi, whose cheeks flushed bright red.

"Geez Andi," Megan whispered, "please tell me you did *something* with all those girls. This isn't exactly wild stuff."

"I was not expecting this from you," she said, her voice a mixture of amusement and vague discomfort.

"Oh, wait, here's the wild stuff," Megan said pulling a set of thick leather handcuffs from a shelf. "Tie someone to a rock with those and then set loose the kraken!"

"I guess so," Andi murmured, refusing to even look.

Megan pulled Andi closer. "I'm not bothering you for real am I?" she whispered, afraid she'd gone too far. "I'm only having a bit of fun."

"No, this is good. Just, I don't know," she blushed. "I'm not quite used to you in this context? So are you into that kind of thing?"

"Honestly," Megan said her voice turning serious, "I don't have the slightest idea."

"So you and your husband never? Played?"

"Well we did have sex," Megan said dryly. "It was just? Uninspired. How about you? You seem a little uncomfortable, but that could mean you don't like this stuff or that you're really really into it."

"It's not my particular thing, but I've had some interesting times. I do have a few of those over there," she pointed, blushing red, at the high-end silicone vibes.

"The purple swan?" Megan asked, her voice a bit giggly.

Andi answered the question by turning beet red and Megan nudged her with her elbow. "Well we have something else in common." The two women laughed at their shared secret as the clerk gave a smirk at them across the shop.

"It's getting late, we should go see Sam."

•••

"There we are," Andi said. A sign at street level announced Venus Gallery & Gifts. At the bottom of the short red brick stairs that led down to the shop's door, Megan paused a moment to look at the framed prints and objects d'art in the plate glass window.

Nervousness set in as Megan opened the door. The shop was more eclectic than she'd expected. Her eye caught a carved and hand painted wooden figure of a woman pirate. It should have been a horrible cliché, but there was something about the pirate's stance and the knowing smirk painted on her face that made it stand out. She'd been afraid it would be a stuffy gallery like the kind she was used to in New York or DC. This was more of a friendly diverse sort of shop and as she scanned the walls looking at her potential competitors, she thought maybe her work might be up to snuff.

"Andi! And you must be Megan the photographer."

"Nice to meet you," Megan said as the woman she assumed was Sam took her hand and shook it firmly. She guessed Sam was more than a few years older as bits of grey were starting to intrude on her spiky black hair and her demeanor had a no nonsense self-assurance that Megan associated with someone who'd had the time to figure themselves out.

"So you're the one who took that picture Andy's using for her Facebook profile?" Sam nodded, apparently sizing Megan up. "It was good. Definitely a step up from the selfie from her phone she had up there before. She sent me a few other things. I like them. Even the ones I can't sell."

Her willingness to get down to business actually calmed Megan. This she understood. "I brought my keeper folder on an iPad. Andi's pic was just a quick shot at the beach really," Megan answered, pulling the tablet from her camera bag and calling up her photos.

"Do you have any thoughts on sale prices or strategies?" the woman asked, looking Megan straight in the eye.

"I'm not sure, I still think of myself as an amateur."

"Well we're more of a consumer shop than fine art. I like to think we are at the high end of what people who aren't collectors are willing to spend. Maybe they want to pick up their first originals. Something to remind them of Provincetown. Something that won't clear out their checking account, but is a step above some generic print from the museum catalog. Looking at what you got here, no offense to Lola, but I can't use dogs. Some of the landscapes are nice, but I don't think for me. I guess this one of the boat would work. I'll have to think. People would be better, particularly if you can tell they're a dyke or you can see Provincetown in the background."

"I don't have anything like that. I've only been here a few weeks. If that's what you're looking for though, I can keep it in mind for my next projects. You know the market and Andi says I can trust you, so I'll go with your advice."

"Well, right now, I'll take the one of the boat and definitely that picture of Andi. Unless, of course, your lovergirl doesn't want to be up on my wall for sale."

Megan and Andi looked at each other. The assumption they were involved spread a wide smile across Megan's face and she gave Andi a quick glance, a bit afraid she'd say something to contradict Sam. "Is that OK?"

"If someone wants to pay to look at me, they badly need to be parted with their money," Andi said looking horribly self-conscious.

•••

"My God Andi, I just sold something," Megan said in a hushed tone, the moment they were out of the shop. "I thought you pitched me. You didn't tell me she was the one who asked about my work!"

"I told you that you were good," Andi replied, her voice nonchalant, but a pleased look on her face. "You're the one who had a hard time believing it."

"I sold a photo! To a gallery!" She was giddy. "I want to do something crazy to celebrate."

"Well, if you want crazy, this is the place. Any ideas of what would that be?" Andi asked.

Megan reached up and gave a tug to one of the captive bead rings in Andi's ear. "I've wanted to get my nose pierced for so long. I just wanted a little stud, nothing scary, but Michael thought it was unprofessional. Is there anyone who does piercing around here?"

"Oh is there ever," Andi laughed. "You will love her!"

•••

Sitting at the table and savoring her meal, Megan had to admit Andi had picked a winner for a restaurant. Their table overlooked the bay and her scallops were as amazing as the view, seared to perfection, delicate and flavorful.

With the sale and Andi's company and the wonderful food and wine, Megan felt content for the first time she could remember. She prodded the left side of her nose, the vague twinge of pain reassuring her that the new piercing was real.

"If you keep jabbing at that, you're just going to make it more sore," Andi said taking a bite of her fish. "She said to leave it alone."

Megan pulled her finger away from the small red gem. "Sorry, I still can't believe I finally did it. I want to touch it to remind myself it's real. If I'd known it was going to be that easy, I'd have gotten one ages ago. What a trip she is."

"Yeah, she's kind of a local legend. Did all of mine. Well, not all, the first pair I got done at the mall like most kids, but the others."

"And would those *others* include anything interesting?" Megan raised an eyebrow.

Andi grinned, "Just what you see. Nothing. Hidden. I am *not* that brave. By the way, the nose thing looks good. It suits you, a little weird, but not too weird."

"Is that what I am? Weird, but not too weird?" Megan asked, tilting her head down in a flirtatious manner.

"I think you're trying to figure out what you are."

The seriousness of the reply took Megan by surprise and she took another sip of the wine and looked out the window at gulls silhouetted against the sunset across Provincetown bay. "Are we going to be serious?"

"Not if you don't want to, it was just what came to mind," Andi smiled.

"I think I'm gay," Megan said. She felt relieved to have it out there, but she still wasn't sure if she was trying it on or making a statement. The more she thought about it, though, the more she felt like it fit her.

"Well, you asked me out on a date, so I kind of thought you might be going there. That wasn't necessarily what I meant about figuring yourself out."

"Sorry, this must seem very silly to you."

"No, you're not being silly. Just take your time," Andi implored, reaching over the table and putting a hand reassuringly on top of Megan's. "It's only been a few weeks since your husband dumped you and you're lonely and stuck here without friends? You have plenty of time to figure it out, you know. You don't have to define anything for yourself. Gay, bi, straight. They're just words."

"Easy for you to say, you had it all figured out so early," Megan said, sounding a bit morose for a dinner that was supposed to be a celebration.

"It was anything but easy."

"I'm sorry," Megan said, clasping Andi's hand. "I know it wasn't. I heard people talking about you. I should have told them to shut up or something. I feel like I turned my back on you."

"You couldn't have done anything and I wasn't exactly being friendly."

Megan knew she was right, but it didn't stop her feeling guilty, particularly as she mulled over her own growing feelings. What if she'd gotten those letters? She was certain it would have changed her life, but what would it have meant to Andi? Would Megan have just been another rich girl summer fling or would it have been more? Was it more now?

"So, no other girls? No lesbian phase in college or anything?" Andi asked.

"None. Well, just seven minutes in heaven with this *really* cute girl when I was thirteen almost fourteen," Megan said, raising her eyebrows and salaciously popping a scallop into her mouth.

"My memory is you weren't exactly shy about it either," Andi said wryly.

"Why waste a good closet," Megan shrugged, feeling a slight blush creep into her cheeks.

"Nobody else?"

"Just guys. A few dates to the movies in high school, Michael in college," she said matter of factly.

"OK, I'll stop picking on you. We should be celebrating, not talking about the past." Andi raised her glass. "To your first gallery sale."

Megan smiled, pride welling up as they clinked glasses and drank.

"The wine is wonderful by the way. So your turn to divulge, how do you know Sam again?" Megan asked.

Andi glanced down at the table nervously. "The wine is one of my favorites."

Megan caught Andi's eyes with her own, letting her know she wasn't going to change the subject quite that easily.

"OK. I used to date this woman Wendy. She and Sam had been involved. They lived together for a while. I met Wendy after they broke up and was at her house when Sam stopped by to drop some things off. You can imagine, she was the last person I wanted to make friends with, but it was like a year later. Wendy and I had broken up and I was here in town and wandered into the gallery. She recognized me and we got to chatting. Had a couple of drinks and toasted our shared mistake. Been friends ever since. Not close, but you know. Facebook friends and I stop in at the shop if I'm in town. That kind of thing."

"Were you and Wendy serious?" Megan winced to herself at the jealous edge in her voice.

"She was serious. I was stupid. She was older. Almost forty. It was my first winter back after college and we fell in together. She'd just broken up with Sam and was looking for something serious. I wasn't. She moved off Cape. Last I heard she was in Jamaica Plain and had gotten married."

"Where'd you go to college?" Megan prayed that Andi hadn't caught the surprised tone in her voice. She hated herself for it, but being raised by a snob like her mother ran deep. She'd just assumed someone doing landscaping hadn't been to school, which was ridiculous because running her own property company may have involved landscaping, but it definitely outranked Megan's record of mindless administrative assistant jobs. Plus Andi's house was full of books and art, why shouldn't she have gone to school?

"U-Mass. The one in Dartmouth for a year, then I transferred out to the Amherst campus. English Lit and Women's Studies."

"English here too!" Megan was delighted to have found something new in common. "Romantic era poetry and Jane Austen and the whole nineteenth century thing."

"Twentieth century realism. If it was about a woman being oppressed, dying in poverty, or best of all *going insane*," Andi made googly eyes as she said the words with emphasis. "I just ate it up."

"Has there been anyone else serious?" Megan changed the subject back.

"Honestly?" Andi's voice was hard to read. "Not really. A few might have gone there eventually, but people our age don't last long on Cape."

"You know how I ended up here. Why'd you move back after school?"

A troubled look flitted across Andi's face for a moment as if the question itself was painful. "It just seemed like the thing to do. The economy was in the toilet, so it wasn't like

I was going to go get a job anywhere else. My parents are older and needed help with the business."

Megan was certain there was something Andi wasn't saying and she opened her mouth to question further, but, thinking better of it, stopped short of actually speaking. They had only reconnected a few brief weeks ago, not quite a month. There was plenty of time.

•••

It was nearly nine when Megan pulled into Andi's driveway and turned off the ignition.

"I had a great time today," Andi said.

Megan felt the same way, but the situation was so silly she almost laughed. Sitting in the car in the dark. The "had a great time" small talk. They could be high school kids with the way they were acting. She certainly felt just as nervous as she ever had on any teenage date. "You know. I've missed this."

"What?"

"The feeling of being with someone you like," Megan squirmed in the car seat to face Andi, "and not knowing what they're thinking or if they like you the same way that you like them."

"Wondering if we're going to kiss goodnight?" Andi asked, the flirty tone in her voice sending Megan's pulse racing.

"That too," she whispered, a nervous anticipation jumping across every nerve as she leaned forward, begging to be kissed. They hesitated a moment, inches away and finally their mouths joined. Andi's lips were so soft, her taste so delicious.

Andi made a tentative nip, her teeth gently biting Megan's lower lip. Their mouths parted and Megan threw her head back laughing "Oh. My. God. It was fifteen years ago and you actually remembered how much that drives me crazy?" Smiling with self-satisfaction, Andi wrapped her hand around Megan's head and pulled her forward, their lips joining together again. Andi's fingers roamed through Megan's hair, taunting the nape of her neck, caressing just so in a way that sent shivers through her entire body.

"You are so delicious," Andi whispered before plunging forward again to devour Megan's lips. "I've wanted to do this since the night you picked up the keys."

"I've wanted to do this again for the last fifteen years," Megan giggled. Barely able to think, she let her hands wander across Andi's waist, caressing the curve of her hipbone through the tight jeans. The steering wheel and gear lever pressed into her body, which only made their fumbling seem furtive and even more delicious, as if they were in high school again and making up for all the lost time.

They reached a pause and came up to breathe, holding each other across the front seats of the car. "I never want this to stop," Megan whispered, gently tugging one of Andi's earrings with her lips.

"I don't either," Andi sighed, "but I think it should."

"Promise we can do it again?" Megan said, licking Andi's neck and savoring the scent of her skin and hair.

"Promise," Andi said and kissed Megan again, their lips sliding together in a slow, deep, romantic caress. As their mouths separated, Andi ran her hand through Megan's hair one last time, gathered herself, and got out of the car. She stood a moment, then leaned back through the open door and touched her finger to the tip of Megan's nose. "And leave that new piercing alone. Don't poke at it."

Chapter 10

As the light filtered in from the spring morning, Megan lay back in the soft sheets and simply smiled. She slept with the window cracked and the room was cold, the air tinged with the vague scent of the ocean. Yes, the beach. The promise of a walk with Andi was the one thing that could make her get out of those warm covers.

She dragged a brush through her hair, reminded once again of why she shouldn't go to bed with her hair wet. After arriving home, she'd hopped in the shower and she and a glass of chardonnay had gone to bed for a little private "Megan time." The unruly locks would have to do. They'd just get blown out in the ocean breeze anyway. She dressed quickly, made up two cups with gobs of sugar and half and half the way Andi liked it and went to her usual perch at the edge of the sand to wait.

A gull had taken over the driveway behind the beach, clutching a clam in its beak, flying thirty or so feet into the air, dropping it onto the small slip of pavement. Dissatisfied with the result, it repeated the process until the hard shell finally broke open and the bird could feast on the meat. It was entertaining enough, but Megan was glad when after a few minutes the figures of a woman and a dog appeared down the beach.

She stood up and plodded through the sand, meeting them halfway. "Fancy running into you two here," she said as they got close enough to hear over the wind.

"An astonishing coincidence," Andi joked.

Megan knelt down and addressed Lola directly. "I have a treat for your girl. Is it OK with you if I give your person a coffee? What? Too much caffeine? But can't she have a treat just this once? Please?"

"Oh give me that. You!" Andi laughed. Megan handed the cup to her then stepped in and offered a kiss as well.

"Oh, sorry Lola, I brought you a biscuit too," she said and pulled out a bone shaped cookie from her pocket.

Andi sipped at her cup, watching them. "I guess this means you don't regret yesterday?"

"Oh tons of regrets, still not sure I should have had the brownie sundae and not the chocolate bread pudding. I also worry the garnet in my nose stud looks too much like a zit, maybe I should have gone for the moonstone? No regrets about you though, if that's what you were asking," Megan sidled up next to her. "You don't? Do you?"

"I just wonder if you're rushing because you think you have to. You don't."

Megan took Andi's arm and pressed close to her as they walked along the shoreline. "Don't worry about me. I know there's lots of evidence to the contrary, but I can take care of myself."

"Speaking of which, stop poking at your nose."

"I'm not poking at it."

"It's red. You're poking at it."

"Miss Andi, it's red because it's a garnet. I am not poking at it," Megan said, her voice filled with faux impatience.

"It doesn't look like a zit, just by the way. It's very pretty."

Megan squeezed her arm and pressed close in appreciation. "I did have an agenda this morning, just so you know."

"And what would that be?" Andi asked.

"I'm wondering what your opinion is of chickens."

"They're fine as long as I don't have to clean the coop. I don't know how your neighbors would feel about a rooster when they're trying to sleep in on summer vacation though."

"Not live chickens," Megan gave her a jab, "roasted ones. Say with garlic and herbs tucked under the skin and a bed of crispy paprika potato wedges?"

"That sounds more promising than cleaning a coop," Andi admitted.

"Well, if you were to show up at my house at say seven o'clock, there just might be one of those chickens *roasting* in its coop."

"Huh," Andi looked at her perplexed.

"Roasting in the oven? Roosting in a coop? Sorry, sometimes I can't help myself. It used to drive Michael crazy. He said I had the humor of a thirteen-year-old."

"As I remember, you were quite a pleasant thirteen year old. Can I bring wine?" Andi asked.

"My inner thirteen-year-old would prefer Diet Coke, but my inner twenty-nine-year-old would be extremely happy if you could find some of that white we were drinking at the restaurant. It would be perfect with chicken."

"Vino Verde. Everyone has it around here. It's Portuguese."

"Of course it is," Megan laughed. "What isn't?"

"It's even cheap," Andi added.

"Great to know I'm a cheap date," Megan quipped, enjoying the banter.

•••

Megan watched as Andi tried to choose between the last two items on her plate, the remaining morsel of chicken or the final crispy red bit of potato. People could *say* they liked your cooking just to be polite, but the way Andi's eyes had widened and the smile that came over her face when she put a bite of food in her mouth? That kind of thing couldn't be faked and it just sent a warm feeling through Megan's soul.

"You're thinking about something." Andi said. It was a statement, not a question.

"Watching you eat reminded me of when my grandmother taught me to cook in the summers I was out visiting here. It wasn't elaborate. I think they would have died if I served them as spicy as those potatoes. I'd make baked cod or just grill a steak or something like that. Then we'd sit down and I could tell how much they enjoyed it. It wasn't much," Megan shrugged, "but it was how we communicated, especially when I got older and could come out without my parents. My mom, she never understood me and cooking or me and anything else really. Making food for someone is important to me, like a way of sharing intimacy."

"Where are your grandparents now? Are they?" Andi let the question trail off.

"No, they're fine. They're in Arizona and show all signs of living forever. They say they're coming up to Cape for a few weeks this summer, but they said that last year too. If they do, it'll be kind of strange, having them as my guests instead of the other way around. What about you?"

"My grandparents passed away. Parents moved to Florida after we sold the cottages. I couldn't see them anywhere else but Cape and I was sure they'd be back within six months, but they seem to like it."

Megan stood and started clearing dishes.

"Can I help you clean up?" Andi asked, not waiting for an answer to start clearing glasses and silverware off the table. The two women made short work of it. "You know," Andi gestured at the dishwasher, "that thing isn't going to get the roasting pan clean."

"I know, but I like to hold onto the fantasy," Megan said mischievously, "and thank you for helping, you really didn't have to."

"I hate not being helpful," Andi said.

"So what now? Movie?" Megan motioned at the living room.

"Sure," Andi said, taking a corner of the couch.

Megan retrieved the remote and sat next to her, leaning back against the other woman and savoring the touch of her body. "Is that OK?"

"It's nice," Andi said putting an arm around Megan's shoulder.

Megan flipped through the offerings on Netflix until they finally settled on a romantic comedy. Megan wasn't concentrating on the movie, not even trying if truth were to be told. All that went through her mind was the presence of this beautiful woman so close, the warmth of her body pressing against her, the gentle weight of her arm around her shoulder.

"Is this movie OK?" she asked.

Andi shifted next to her, "it's fine, OK for you?"

Megan turned her head. Even in the dim light, Andi's eyes were so beautifully blue. "I don't care about the movie," she admitted and moved closer. Hesitating a moment, Megan saw a glance of assent and pressed her lips against Andi's. Would she ever tire of the softness of her mouth? The touch of her tongue?

Breaking their kiss, Megan leaned back, pulling Andi on top of her. "I want you."

Andi reached out and cupped Megan's head in one hand, the other caressing her hip. She leaned over and captured Megan's mouth once again. She was relentless, her tongue lashing out, their lips pressing together hard and firm.

Running her hands across Andi's backside, Megan took delight at the other woman's response at her touch. Feeling bolder, she put a hand on Andi's shirt, tracing her fingers gently across the soft fabric. There was no hint of a bra and she could feel the pebbled nipple beneath her fingers. She began to hastily unsnap buttons and slid her hand into Andi's shirt.

Touching another woman's breast was more than Megan had ever imagined it would be. She cupped the soft warm orb, exploring its warm roundness, and eliciting a sigh of pleasure from Andi. Touching her made Megan tremble with need stronger than anything she'd ever experienced. She could feel wet arousal spreading, her clit throbbing, the intensity of her desire so overwhelming. Why had she wasted so much time before realizing sex could be this good?

Megan tweaked the stiff nub of the nipple between her fingertips, but instead of the mewling responses she'd been expecting, Andi's hands withdrew from her hips and she pulled her body away, crossing her arms in front of her. Megan tried to meet her eyes, searching for some explanation, but Andi was simply looking away, staring into space.

"What's wrong?" Megan's distress was clear in her voice.

"I'm sorry," Andi's voice was distant, like she was a million miles away. "I don't think we should do this."

"Well this is a hell of a time to come to that conclusion," Megan said, hurt mixing with impatience and frustration. Her body demanded satisfaction and her soul craved connection with the gorgeous woman still straddling her hips. "What am I doing wrong? Don't you like me?"

"Nothing. You're everything right," Andi wiped a tear from her eye. "I just don't want to push you."

"You are *not* pushing me," Megan said firmly.

"You need to slow down and think about this," Andi rolled off of her, sitting on the opposite end of the couch.

"Don't tell me what I need to do," Megan growled, anger welling up. "I have had more than enough of people telling me what to do. I know what I want and I want you."

"You don't know what you want. You're lonely. You're hurt. I'm here and I don't want you to mistake that for attraction."

"Don't you dare," Megan barked, her mouth running on its own. "I'm tired of other people thinking they know what's best for me. My mother pushing me at Michael. Him pushing me at law school and all those fucking political cocktail parties and that crap. I am exactly where I want to be tonight with exactly who I want to be with."

Andi slid off the couch and stood casting her eyes down at Megan. "I just don't want to hurt you. I need to go."

"Please? Stay?" Megan watched in horror as Andi fastened the buttons on her shirt. "We don't have to do anything. We could just talk. We could watch the movie. Please." Andi didn't answer and taking her jacket quietly slipped out the door. As it shut behind her, Megan broke down, tears flowing down her face and her body convulsing with sobs.

Chapter 11

There wasn't even the hint of sunrise through the window as Megan turned and grabbed the phone off her nightstand. *Keep telling yourself it's to check the time,* she thought as it flickered to life bringing disappointment when there were no new emails or texts. 3:42 a.m. Twenty two minutes after the last time she'd picked it up to look. That made, two, almost three hours of tossing sleeplessly. Closing her eyes, she rolled onto her back, straightening her body, trying to find a position that would let her actually rest.

When the first light started to peek into the window an hour later, she surrendered and sat up. The rounded posts and thick footboard caught her eye and she flashed back to her and Andi struggling to get it through the door. "Ugh," she said to the emptiness and slid her feet onto the floor.

On autopilot, she grabbed a robe and made her way downstairs, set up the coffee to run, went back up and turned on the shower. After a night of mulling over her fight with Andi rather than sleeping, she could feel the fatigue oozing out of her skin. She stepped under the hot needles of water, hoping they might restore some semblance of functionality.

Dressing quickly, trying to beat the sun, she poured the usual two cups of coffee, dosed them with cream and sugar, and headed out into the early morning. Even in the twilight, it was obviously going to be a wonderful day, unseasonably warm and only a few wispy clouds. Once she was clear of the cottages, she looked down the beach. An older couple was walking down near the water, but no sign of Andi and Lola.

Megan sat and drank her coffee as the sun slowly crept over the horizon. "What do you think?" Megan asked the gull perched a few feet down from her. It opened its yellow beak and cocked its head in answer, eyeing her suspiciously. "Yeah, I was afraid of that."

She took out her phone for what must have been the tenth time since arriving and confirmed she'd been waiting for over an hour. Andi was never this late, particularly since it had become a daily ritual. No messages. No texts. "Send her another message?" Megan questioned her feathered companion. The white bird unfolded its wings and leapt into the air. "Thanks a lot gull."

An hour after getting home, she finally overcame her nervousness and texted. *Missed you at the beach. Miss you period.* She held the phone for five minutes, waiting for a response, and felt foolish when none came. What had she done? This was ridiculous.

A clean kitchen, vacuumed living room, and changed bed later, her phone finally beeped with an incoming text.

Took Lola to the dog park.

She stared vacantly at the message, but no matter how many times she read it, the words didn't change. It was so barren of any emotion or intimacy. If Andi hadn't wanted this, why had she agreed to come over? Why had she stayed after dinner? The events raced through Megan's mind again, replaying like a bad video, but there were still no clues. One moment the joy of being together and the pleasure of melding bodies. The next moment emptiness.

You have to talk to me sometime.

This time the answer from Andi came quickly. *Port Cafe 1:00 p.m.?*

I'll see you there, Megan answered.

•••

"Sorry I'm late," Andi said as she sat down. I got hung up with a customer. She's old and lonely and just wanted to talk and I didn't want to be rude."

Megan appreciated the apology. She'd been nursing the red plastic glass of Diet Coke and mentally tracing patterns in the linoleum floor for nearly a half hour. "That's fine. I know you're busy. It's nice you take time for customers like that. It's hard not having someone." Megan knew that wasn't playing fair, but it seemed to have the desired effect. Andi stopped nervously fingering the menu and their eyes met. They were still the same beautiful blue, but they didn't seem to hold any answers today.

"Hey you two," the waitress said pulling out an order pad, "what can I get you?"

"Club sandwich plate on wheat toast. And coffee," Andi said, putting the menu back.

"And you?"

Megan hadn't bothered with a menu. "Fries I guess? Small fries?"

"Come on, you have to eat something," Andi said.

"Just the fries," Megan said, mortified at arguing in front of the waitress. They had barely said hello, when had this become an argument? Or maybe how was a better question.

Megan watched as Andi sat back and shifted uncomfortably in her seat, fidgeting with a fork. "Talk to me?" she gasped out, her attempt at not sounding desperate failing utterly.

Andi looked out the window rather than meeting her eyes. "It's my fault and I apologize. I should never have let things get out of hand."

"I don't think they were out of hand at all," Megan insisted.

"But they are out of hand. You're married."

"We're divorcing."

Andi sighed, "But you're not divorced yet."

"Not convincing Andi," Megan muttered. "In every way that counts, I'm completely free. The agreements are signed; it's only a matter of the waiting period. He and Miss Thing have even been at a fundraiser for her father."

"You've never been with other women, how do you even know you're gay?" Just as she said this, the waitress returned with their food and they fell silent. Megan could see the waitress' eyes glancing back and forth and made a note to leave a big tip. She didn't need to see this kind of drama. "You need to take a step back and think about all this," Andi continued as the waitress left.

"I know how I feel when I'm with you." Megan held out her hand, but Andi picked up a French fry rather than taking it. "I know that you leaving last night was more devastating than when Michael told me he wanted a divorce."

"See, that's it. You're lonely and on the rebound and I'm concerned you're confused by it all."

"I thought you were the one who told me not to worry about defining myself. I think I'm gay, but even if I'm not, I care about you. I think you feel the same. Isn't it enough?"

"It never has been," Andi cast her eyes down at the table and took an unhappy bite of her sandwich.

Megan didn't have an answer to that and picked at a French fry. It was perfect, tasty, and crisp; but she didn't have any real appetite. "If you felt that way, why did you let us get close?"

"I liked you Megan."

The past tense in her statement was like a dagger. "Liked?"

"Liked. Like. I don't know. I know this is a bad idea, no matter what you feel or I feel or we think we feel. You don't need the complications in your life and neither do I."

"You are not a complication," her resistance dazed Megan. "You are the best thing that's ever happened to me."

Andi seemed to wince at the words, but she remained resolute, "I just don't think this is a good idea. I'm sorry I let it get this far."

"Look at me," Megan said, trying to keep her voice steady. "Look me in the eye and tell me you don't care about me."

Andi glanced up for a moment, but wouldn't meet Megan's eyes. "I'm sorry," she shook her head and leaving her food barely touched, laid a twenty-dollar bill on the table and got up.

"Please," Megan turned, her eyes following as Andi shuffled out to the sidewalk.

Chapter 12

Megan heard the phone ringing across the room where she'd left it. Convinced that Andi had finally come to her senses, she abandoned the rerun she was watching and leapt up from the couch to grab it before it went to voice mail. "Hello?"

"Megan?" the voice while vaguely familiar wasn't Andi's.

"Yes, this is Megan."

"This is Samantha, from Venus Gallery. I haven't heard from you so I wanted to give you a call."

Megan cringed. She'd made a mental note to get the prints made, but she just hadn't gotten around to it. First, she needed to figure out where she was ordering them from. As she held the phone, trying to think of an excuse, she noticed the dishes on the counter. She hadn't gotten around to much and needed to stop… Stop doing what exactly? Doing nothing? Wallowing? "Sorry, it hasn't been the best week," she said, not sure what else she could say.

"Andi didn't fuck things up with you two did she?"

Well that was blunt, Megan thought, not sure she wanted to talk about this with someone she'd only met for a fifteen-minute sales pitch. On the other hand, maybe Sam had some idea what was going on.

"Well that silence answers that one," Sam said over the phone, her voice sounding disgusted. "Look, I would like your prints if you're still interested. It's also Single Women's Weekend coming up. Come out here. Take some pictures for me."

"I wasn't sure if you'd still want to buy anything. You know? If you were just taking them as a favor because I knew Andi."

"No, I want them because I can sell them. Real estate is too expensive in this town to take up space on my wall with favors for a friend."

Well that was something. Knowing it was her talent and not just a favor gave Megan the first emotional boost she'd had in days. She hesitated for a moment, unsure if she shouldn't leave the talk at the professional level, and then roused the courage to ask. "I like Andi. I don't want to ask you to say anything you don't think you should, but you were awful fast to ask if something happened. Is there something I should know? I'd like to, maybe, try to fix things?"

"Nobody can fix anyone but themselves," Sam said bluntly. "That's something we all have to learn. As to Andi, let's say she has a habit of going all cut and run when someone turns out to be for real. She has her reasons, but I don't think it's for me to say what they are. You might give her some time and ring her up. She might listen. On the other hand, if she doesn't feel like listening, there's going to be a few thousand horny girls your age and a little younger in town this weekend. Maybe you should just get laid."

"I'll take that under advisement," Megan said hoping to be a bit humorous and eliciting a huge laugh from Sam. Megan wondered if there was something she was missing out on in the conversation. She was glad that Sam shared her sense of humor, but it wasn't all that funny. On the other hand, feeling as if she didn't quite understand things was something she'd been fighting with ever since she crossed the bridge onto Cape.

After they hung up, Megan pulled out her laptop and started setting up the print order. The picture haunted her. There was Andi, staring at her from the screen, captured forever. For a moment, she thought of calling Sam back and canceling so she could keep the image only for herself. No, pining away with her photo seemed a little too gothic novel at best and plain pathetic at worst. She paged through the other photos remembering those mornings on the beach and found one of Lola mercilessly tormenting a stick as a wave crashed around her. *Why not*, she thought and added an 8x10. She could at least leave Andi with a souvenir.

●●●

"Nice camera," the redhead said. Megan had been sitting on one of the benches in the center of Provincetown, taking discreet shots of anyone who appeared interesting when the other woman had sat down next to her, a little closer than someone who wanted to remain a stranger would. "Shooting street photography?"

"Drat, you caught me," Megan joked, surprised at the flirtatious tone in her own voice. "So was that just a line or are you interested in photography?"

"A little bit of both?" she cast a sexy smile at Megan. "I'm Emily, but most people call me Em."

"Megan," she said, feeling just a little wary.

"Is that the X100?"

"Yup, the new model," Megan answered. "It's perfect for this. If you recognize it, I guess you *do* know something about photography."

"Just a little gear lust. I have an older camera I got used. Well I have it, but not with me. Would it be terrible if I asked if I could check out yours?"

"Sure," Megan smiled and handed the faux-vintage silver and black camera over. While the girl, Em, was playing with controls and such, Megan took the opportunity to give her a second look. She was young, but dressed a little more maturely than the packs of college babydykes wandering Commercial Street, so maybe twenty-four or twenty-five? *Not too young for me.* Where had that come from? Light hazel eyes and freckled skin pale enough that her insanely red hair might actually be natural. Her face was soft and bright and she was all smiles and Megan had to admit to herself that she found her very pretty.

"Wow, I'd love to have a piece of kit like that," she said handing the camera back. "I don't suppose you'd like to move this a little down the road and have a drink with me?"

Megan froze, not because she didn't want to, but because she realized she did. Andi was wrong that their attraction was simply loneliness, but that didn't mean spending so much time alone was any fun. It would be nice to share a drink and talk about photography or whatever even if she had no intention of sleeping with Em or anyone else. At least not today.

"We could scout out a place where you can take pictures of people when they walk by? Or I know a place with pretty drinks; you could take pictures of them? Come on? I won't bite."

"I guess," Megan gave a pursed lip smile before capitulating. "I'll be honest though, I'm just here taking pictures. I'm really not looking for anyone."

Em gave her a flirty look up and down. "Does that mean I can't try to convince you that finding someone would be a good idea?"

"You can try," Megan said looking at her straight in the eyes. Damn they were pretty. What was it about women's eyes?

"I can live with that," Em said with a flirty toss of her red hair and a smile that made it obvious she had every intention of trying.

As they walked up the street, the crowd parted as a red Mini Cooper convertible, top down with four cute girls inside, drove slowly up the center of Commercial Street. This weekend was a younger crew with more women than the last time Megan had visited. Had it only been two weeks ago? They'd been so happy. Thinking about it, she realized it had only been a month and a half since she'd arrived on Cape, thinking of it as an exile.

"So where are you from?" Em's question pulled Megan out of her thoughts.

Megan grinned at her. "This seems funny to say, but I actually live on Cape. Down in Dennisport. You?"

"Oh," Em sounded surprised. "I guess I figured everyone was here for the weekend. I'm from Quincy, but I'm staying just outside of town in Truro." Em clearly had a destination and they were soon sitting at a quiet table with drinks ordered.

"Photography's your hobby?" Em asked.

"I got my first real camera a few years ago as a gift and took a couple of courses and got hooked. Actually, do you know the Venus Gallery?"

"Other end of town? Down near the bookstore?"

"That's the one," Megan smiled. "It was the owner's idea for me to come out this weekend. She bought one of my photos and thought I could get some shots with all the women in town."

"Grats girl! Are they in the shop? I'd love to see your work."

"I'm waiting for prints, but here," Megan paged through her phone, "this is the one she bought."

"Beautiful."

"She is."

Em raised her eyes, "I meant the photo, but she is too. A little butch for me, I'm more into, well, your type. I'm guessing she's also the reason you're not looking to hook up with anyone?"

"Guilty," Megan said. "I did warn you."

"Girlfriend?"

"Not quite and currently broken up sort of?"

"Only sort of?" Em leaned back and looked around the room, "let's order some food and you can tell me the story."

Chapter 13

Megan sat on the couch, the small computer perched on her lap, thinking to herself that she needed a larger screen if she was going to be doing this much photography. Nevertheless, her visit to Provincetown had yielded several images she thought might be good enough to sell. The laptop came to life and she ran the email program. Even after this time, she still had a twinge of disappointment when there was nothing from Andi.

> Sam.
>
> I will have the prints of the Andi/Beach photo for you. I took your advice about shooting this weekend and am forwarding some of what I think are the stronger pieces. Please let me know if there is interest so I can get them printed ASAP.
>
> Megan

It was a few hours later when the answer came.

> I knew the weekend would inspire you. I'll send a list of which ones I want, but I particularly think the one of the two girls is stunning. If you can have them done for Memorial Day, would you be available Sunday afternoon for a wine and cheese thing?
>
> Sam

Megan knew right away the shot she meant. She'd seen two girls, college kids probably, looking completely smitten and had captured them sharing a quick kiss. What made the picture was the unhappy straight couple behind them, barely in focus. The contrast between the happiness of the two women and the disgruntled look on the man's face spoke volumes particularly when sharpened by the stark black and white.

The first round of prints was already mounted and framed. The lab had done a great job of printing and thanks to instructions courtesy of Google, framing had been easier than she'd feared. Sitting among the larger pieces, there was the odd print out. The picture of Lola frolicking on the beach standing out both because of its smaller size and color printing. Megan wasn't sure what masochistic tendency had led her to leave it propped up where she could see it every time she walked through the house. *Maybe I could put it in the closet,* she morbidly laughed to herself. *Or maybe I should get out more and stop rattling around this house.*

Mail it? Drop it off and try to be casual? Andi could ignore the gesture if she just sent it in the mail, but showing up might make her freak out again. Drop it off, she finally decided. Definitely drop it off and no better time than the present. She wrapped it in pages from the local newspaper and grabbed her keys.

When she pulled her wagon into Andi's driveway, she didn't see the Subaru or the trailer. She wondered if she should come back another time, but the thought of driving by until Andi was home seemed more than a little like stalker behavior. Even dropping it off was bad enough. She rifled through her purse, found a piece of paper, and jotted off a quick note. "I was getting the prints made for Sam's shop and saw this and thought you might like it. I hope you are well—Megan" Oh God, "hope you are well?" Did she really write that? Damn. She searched again, but it was the only thing she had to write on so she was stuck with it. She tucked it into the package, left it inside the screen door, and beat a hasty retreat.

•••

Under the cool grey skies, Megan wove through the Provincetown crowd. She had no doubt the Business Association would have dialed up a nicer weekend if they could, but it hadn't seemed to deter the crowds. She laughed to herself that even Andi would have gladly paid for parking. If Andi was here, which she wasn't. The weather was a shame, it had been beautiful and warm when she dropped the prints off Tuesday, but by the weekend, the temperature had dipped down to the 50s and clouds had overtaken the sky.

When she walked through the door, her eyes locked on the four photographs on the wall. Her photographs. She stopped dead in her tracks and stared as the reality set in. *Her photography was on the wall of a gallery.* Her own visage was there as well, on a small laminated card under them. "Don't faint on me," Sam said, strolling over from behind a display and putting a friendly arm around her, "it'll cost both of us money if you do. Not to mention being embarrassing."

"It doesn't seem real," Megan whispered.

"Just imagine how real it will be to deposit the checks," Sam replied conspiratorially, "and have a glass of wine, it'll loosen you up."

Sam introduced Megan to the two other artists, a potter and a painter whose work was also being showcased and then she mingled, gradually losing the feeling of being a poser as she answered questions. After an hour of working the crowd, Megan was taking a moment to look at the painter's work as well as contemplating how sore her feet were when she felt a hand on her shoulder. "Hey baby." Megan turned around and found herself face to face with

Emily, her hazel eyes locked on Megan's. "Congratulations on the big time show."

"How did you?" Megan stuttered out, delighted to see the redhead.

"You didn't think I was going to let you bend my ear over drinks and not see you again did you?"

"Wow," Megan mumbled.

"Wow?" Em giggled.

"I just didn't expect to ever see you again," Megan said taking Em's hand.

"Well, I asked Sam about you and she said to sign up for the newsletter, there would probably be a showing sometime. So here we are."

"Here we are," Megan repeated nervously. Andi hadn't even acknowledged the print she'd left, much less answered any of her emails or texts. Megan didn't owe her anything and she liked Em. She was attractive and available and right in front of her and obviously more than mildly interested. Did she make Megan's heart flutter the way Andi had? No, the truth was she didn't. Could she? Maybe?

"Well," Em squeezed her hand, "if you have time and wouldn't mind my company, I'd love to take you out for dinner to celebrate."

Megan gazed at the smile on her face. Em was obviously smitten and hard to resist all things considered.

"It's just dinner," Emily's eyes pled with her.

"Sure, that would be great," Megan said as a wave of relief flooded over her.

"Well, I don't want to distract you from your public and I don't think I can stop myself from monopolizing your time. Remember the place we got drinks? How about you meet me there when you're done here?" Em gave her hand another squeeze before relinquished it.

"Sure, I'll meet you there," Megan said, "I think I have an hour left."

Megan watched Em leave the shop, she felt a little guilty for doing so, but couldn't help noticing how pleasant the curve of Em's backside looked in the tight jeans she was wearing.

"Friend?" Sam asked.

"Another photographer. We met on Single Women's Weekend."

"I have to admit, I thought Andi would show," Sam said.

"She hasn't even sent a text, why would she show up here?" Megan's voice was glum at the reminder.

"I thought she'd show up because I yelled at her for an hour. Sorry if that was meddling in your business, but she needs to get over herself. I'm tired of watching her screwing up good things."

Megan thought a moment, not sure if she was thankful or horrified at the thought of other people stepping into their relationship problems, but decided it was meant well. "That's alright. If it had worked, I would have been very grateful."

"Well, if I read people well, you have someone interested and she's cute. What's her name?"

"Emily," Megan replied, "or rather Em."

"Well good for you. By the way, I already have orders and those two older women don't know it yet, but they are going to buy as soon as they have a chance to get to know you. So back to work. Schmooze! Schmooze! Schmooze!"

•••

The cheese was dwindling and Sam had stopped refilling the carafe of wine from the box in the back room. Megan glanced at her watch, anxious to stop being on display. It seemed rude to leave while there were still people who might want to talk to her and she was hoping for a lull, so she could sneak out while the gallery was empty. How was it possible that just chatting with people could be so exhausting? Her hopes of escaping where crushed when the door opened once again.

Megan turned to the door and felt like she'd been punched in the gut. Tall with that sandy blond hair and that western shirt that looked so good on her. It was Andi. Megan took a deep breath and looked her over. It was silly, but she expected her to look different. It had been two weeks, not two years, but it felt like everything that had happened should have some physical manifestation.

"Hey," Andi said, her demeanor so hesitant Megan thought she might turn and run out of the gallery at any moment.

Megan tried to read what Andi might be thinking. Above the shock of seeing her again, Megan realized there was another feeling welling up: anger. "Hello," she said, her voice pure ice.

"Congratulations on the show. Those are yours?" she indicated the new photos that Megan had taken after their fight.

"Yes. I took them a few weeks ago. The Single Women's Weekend thing."

"I'm sorry," Andi said. "I would like to talk."

"I don't think this is the best time," Megan snapped back, surprised at herself. She was seething. She'd had these romantic fantasies about reuniting with Andi, but for Megan the reality was all rage. *How dare she?* Megan felt like she'd just managed to get her legs back and now everything was rocking again.

Andi glanced down at the hardwood floor of the gallery and wiped her eye to wipe away an incipient tear.

"Maybe after your show? We could get dinner somewhere? Or a drink?"

"Look. I might call you," Megan took a breath and tried not to sound quite so angry. "I *will* call you. We need to talk. But not today. I already have a date."

Andi's usually ruddy face drained pale.

Megan took a petty satisfaction in surprising her. "And for your information, my date is with another woman. So you can stop worrying about the 'not gay' stuff."

Andi nodded. "Is she someone serious?" she asked, her voice sounding terrified.

"Actually, she's kind of lighthearted, you might take a hint," Megan knew as she said it that she'd given up any pretense at righteous anger and moved on to pure bile. "Oh God, I'm sorry. No, it could be more, but right now we're just friends."

The relief on Andi's face spoke volumes to Megan. After two weeks of silence, Megan had started to lose hope that Andi had ever cared for her, much less ever would again. She'd started to write off the time they spent together as a misunderstanding, but clearly there was something there. While she wasn't going to give her any slack today, there was no question in Megan's mind that she'd forgive almost anything if they could be together.

•••

Em was perched at a corner table reading a book, a basket of bread and half-drained martini her only company. Megan wasn't sure the walk over had been enough to compose herself after encountering Andi, but it was too late to change her mind. Em had caught a glance of her and was beaming.

"Hi hi!" Em said, as Megan hung her jacket on the chair and sat down. "How was the rest of the show?"

"It was confusing," Megan said, opting for honesty. She knew this wasn't going to be a pleasant conversation, but she was a lousy liar and would never be able to bluff through dinner. "The show went great, but Andi showed up at the end."

Em's smile faded noticeably. "And?"

"I wasn't kind," Megan admitted, "but I just don't know. I'm sorry. I don't think playing advice columnist again was what you had in mind for tonight."

Em took her hand, tracing her fingertips over Megan's knuckles. "Look, you're beautiful. I'd be lying if I denied the idea of you taking me back to Dennis and doing the horizontal bop wasn't a pleasant one, but if that doesn't happen, I'm not going to have a broken heart or something. I am quite capable of being friends with or without benefits."

"Thanks. I think today I could use a friend more than the horizontal bop."

"Are you going to give her another chance?" Em asked, sipping her drink.

"I never even thought of it that way. I only thought about getting her back, but when I saw her I went all Ellen Ripley on her. I was so angry. Just so... so pissed off. I'm afraid I used our dinner date as a weapon."

"I don't mind. I've always wanted to be a human weapon. Maybe I played X-Box too much with my brother?"

Megan laughed.

"See, you still have a sense of humor. Don't worry about it. What you need to worry about is whether you want your lobster boiled or baked stuffed and whether you're getting chowder or bisque."

"Eat my emotions? I'm good with that."

Chapter 14

Megan had gone over it in her mind again and again over the past two days. She knew exactly what she wanted to say, but when the knock came on the door, her well planned words evaporated in a cloud of panic. Hand trembling on the doorknob, she took a deep breath and opened the door.

"Hi Andi, come on in," she said.

"Hey," Andi responded contritely and stepped in, looking around the room as if it was her first time visiting.

"Sit down," Megan said gesturing at the living room. "I have a couple of steaks for dinner, good ones from the Village Market."

"Anything is great."

Megan retrieved a bottle of merlot and two glasses from the kitchen and took a seat opposite Andi. "You know what pissed me off the most?" Andi visibly recoiled, but Megan couldn't contain herself. "You always seemed so in control and you acted like this. If you didn't want a relationship with me, it would have been so easy to tell 'the straight girl' to leave you alone. Why didn't you just do that?"

"I want a relationship with you," Andi said. "You are beautiful and smart and I love being around you. I thought you would be better off if you didn't get involved right now, particularly with a woman."

"Lay off that shit Andi," Megan sniped exasperated. "I have no idea what's going on, but the one thing I've figured out is this isn't about me. It's about you."

Chastened, Andi sat quietly for what seemed like an eternity. "Maybe I should go."

"Oh please," Megan sighed, rubbing her eyes. "Don't run away again. Talk to me."

"I don't know what to say."

"Andi. I have known you since I was thirteen. I didn't even know that funny feeling was attraction the first time we met. I felt the same attraction when I was picking up the keys to this place before I even knew it was you. I don't know what it is about you, but it's there. It can't be a one-way street though. I had that with Michael. I'm not doing that again."

"People leave," Andi said sadly. It seemed like she thought the meaning was obvious, but it escaped Megan's grasp.

"People stay too. I'd like to stay."

"I've heard that before Megan. I've heard how those summer girls were going to write to me. I heard it from my college girlfriend before she moved to California. I heard it from women who moved here and were going to stay, then got in their cars and left the first day in September that the temperature went below sixty. I've heard it from straight girls who were straight until they weren't, then suddenly they were again."

"I'm sorry that happened to you, but it's no excuse to treat me the way you have," Megan insisted.

"It's not an excuse for walking out like I did and I apologize, but it is a reason I'm the way I am." Andi twisted her fingers together, her eyes cast downward, unwilling to meet Megan's. "I'm tired of getting excited about someone and ending up waving goodbye to them."

"Please look at me?" Megan pled. Andi raised her head, her eyes blurry with barely held back tears. "I'm scared too. I may not show it, but trust me, I'm very aware you're a woman and even if I'm enthusiastic, being with another woman is scary as hell when I think about it."

"I would like to try again, if you are willing to give me another chance." Andi's voice was piteous and small.

Megan scanned her looking for some clue as to whether this was for real or not. She ached to reach out, wrap her arms around Andi, and forgive it all, but she wasn't sure that was the best thing for either of them. She wanted Andi to be happy and she was afraid she might not be enough to make that happen.

"I can't promise this will last forever, but I can promise I am in this for real. I'm not just playing or experimenting or something. Cape? I don't know. It's lonely here, but whatever we do, we'll talk about that when the time comes. Would that work? Just taking things one step at a time?" Megan offered.

"I can do that," Andi said, relief washing over her features, reminding Megan of how beautiful she was.

"We could start with dinner. I hope my no good caretaker made sure the propane for the grill was filled."

Andi blushed. "I'm afraid the no good caretaker didn't check the grill, but we can take a look."

•••

"The steaks were pretty awesome. Thank you for taking over cooking," Megan said.

Andi shrugged. "Let the grill heat up first and only turn them once. There's not much to it. Simple is best."

"Well, I appreciate it anyway," Megan said, getting up from the table. Cooking and eating together had been a nice relief from the intensity of their earlier conversation and without thinking she gave Andi a quick peck on the cheek while taking her plate. She glanced back at the table and saw an appreciative smile from the tall blond, reminding her of everything that had attracted her in the first place.

Andi got up and joined her to help with the dishes, sending a nervous twinge creeping up Megan's spine. This was almost exactly a rerun of that terrible night. After this, they'd sit on the couch and turn on the TV and then what? The physical attraction was still there, a persistent if gentle pull of desire, but it was mixed with a fear Andi might bolt again.

"I have some ice cream, if you'd like to stay and maybe watch some TV and have dessert?"

Andi looked at her and with a worried smile nodded. "I'd like that very much."

"Chocolate or vanilla?" Megan asked, waving two cartons in the air.

"You gotta ask?" Andi gave her a look.

"OK, chocolate. It's always good to ask though. Go sit down and relax," Megan laughed.

Ice cream scooped and in hand, Megan sat down on the couch. "Here you are," she offered one of the heaping bowls. Was it Megan's imagination or had Andi moved a little away? As they ate, Megan studied her face. Andi's eyes darted around, from the bowl, to a quick glance at Megan, to the room around. Was she letting her fears run wild or did Andi's smile seem ever so slightly forced. "Any idea what you'd like to watch?" Megan asked trying to spur conversation.

"I missed you," Andi said, her voice both serious and sincere.

"Same," Megan's voice was barely a whisper.

"No, not only when we had the fight," Andi continued. "Before then. When I was at home. Or working. I missed you all the time. Every morning I looked forward to seeing you on the beach. It scared the shit out of me. I don't like being dependent."

"That's not being dependent, that's what falling for someone is about," Megan put down her now empty bowl and placed a hand gently on Andi's shoulder.

"I don't want to lose myself. Heartbreaks are one thing, but Wendy was worse than any of the times people just left. My college girlfriend had dumped me and I moved back here and I fell hard, but it was like my whole personality just got consumed, like a vampire or something. My fault as well as hers, but that just makes me even more cautious. Or scared."

Megan nodded silently, letting Andi talk. She'd known there was more to the Wendy thing.

"Looking back, I get it now. She was insecure and wanted things and we were in different places in life. She pushed here and there and I was in over my head and just going along with what Wendy wanted. Sam talked sense into me before we got married or had a kid or something I couldn't walk away from. That's part of why we're friends."

"That sounds strangely familiar," Megan said.

"Oh?"

"Sort of how I ended up on Cape in the first place? My roommate Elissa tried to talk sense into me, but my mother kept pushing."

"Like those old cartoons with the angel and devil on someone's shoulder?"

"I'm not sure Elissa was exactly an angel," Megan giggled, thinking of their various drunken adventures. "She wants to meet you by the way. My mother as a devil though? That's one I can go along with." Megan gave her a lighthearted nudge on the shoulder, rose, and took their bowls into the kitchen. Quickly rinsing them, she returned to the living room and turned the lights down. "What are we watching?"

"Honestly, I could use something stupid. Stupid and funny," Andi said.

"Romantic comedy?" Megan said, sitting and leaning her body into Andi's

"Give me the remote," Andi had a conspiratorial smirk on her face. "I want to see if they have something for streaming."

"What?"

"They do have it! How about a silly sexy *lesbian* romantic comedy?"

"Oh that does sound good," Megan said.

"Oh, it is," Andi said wrapping her arm around Megan's shoulders.

●●●

"Oh my God, that kiss," Megan pressed her body against Andi's, soaking in her warmth.

"You liked the movie?"

"You have to ask? Obviously. I didn't think anything so wacky could be so romantic."

"We'll have to go through my lesbian DVD collection, but right now, I guess I should go," Andi gently traced her fingertips across Megan's neck.

Megan sighed, not wanting the night to end. "It's late, you could stay here. I mean, we could just sleep. It doesn't have to even be the same bed."

"Tempting, but Lola's waiting up for me," Andi said. "She'd probably like to take a little walk around the yard."

"She's always welcome here, you know that?"

Andi stroked Megan's shoulder. "I'm guessing that means I'm welcome too?"

"You are," Megan softly pressed her lips against Andi's cheek. "You are always welcome."

●●●

An hour before dawn, Megan woke easily, a smile cemented onto her face. Looking outside the window, the beginnings of light morning fog drifted through the yard. She checked theweather report on her phone. Sun should burn it off. She showered and went quickly through the practiced ritual of making two cups of coffee. Balancing them in one hand, she opened the door, only to be met by a happy blur of black and brown fur yipping at her feet. "Lola?"

"Don't knock her over, you crazy dog! That's my coffee!" Andi's voice rang out.

"I guess we both had the same idea," Megan smiled.

"Thought I'd surprise you. Did it work?" Andi looked almost ludicrously satisfied with herself as she stood at the bottom of Megan's stairs.

"Have a coffee you," Megan handed her the cup, reveling in the pleasant back and forth.

Lola yipped for attention, pulling at the leash, anxious to get out to the beach. The two women quietly acquiesced to the demands of the terrier and let her lead them through the cottage colony pathway to the ocean. Stepping over the cement barrier onto the sand, a gull hovered ten feet away, swooped up a few feet, and landed with a flourish sending Lola into a frenzy.

"I don't think Mr. Gull is impressed," Megan noted and reaching into her pocket, pulled out a scrap of bread and tossed it to the bird. It cocked its head looking at her, swooped down to grab the crust, and leapt back into the air to find a quieter place to eat.

"God don't feed those things. They're like flying rats."

"I still think they're pretty," Megan teased, knowing her affection for the creatures drove Andi crazy.

Andi took a sip of her coffee and shook her head. "Feathered cockroaches. You'll get over it when you've lived here a few years. Now that we have our coffee on, could I convince you to let me make you breakfast?"

"You certainly can," Megan replied, taking Andi's arm.

They made their way down the shore, Lola delighting in barking until any nearby terns or gulls took to the air. Now Memorial Day was past, the summer proper had begun and they no longer had the early morning beach to themselves. There were even a few brave souls in bathing suits, clearly there to make a day of it. Andi led them off the sand to a gravel paved lane, then down a trail through a sparse copse of trees to her cottage.

"Home again, home again, jiggety jig," Andi announced opening the door. "I hope you're hungry, I did a little shopping at the Farmer's Market yesterday. Fresh local eggs, Irish breakfast sausage and thick cut bacon from a little farm in Yarmouth, and I picked up some Portuguese sweet bread at the bakery, thought I'd make French toast with it."

"That's not breakfast, that's a feast," Megan grinned, walked over, and putting her hands on Andi's hips, kissed her. "So pretty and you cook too?" she whispered.

"Hey, this is the second time I've cooked you breakfast," Andi said, pulling Megan into a hug.

"I seem to remember the last time was instant oatmeal, but the hangover has left that day a little fuzzy though."

"There was toast too."

"Oooh, toast! You'll be the next Top Chef, you goof," Megan gave Andi a bump with her hip. "Is there something I can help with?"

"You can sit down and I'll pour you some orange juice."

"From the local orange groves of Dennis?"

"Fresh squeezed from the carton," Andi said, pouring a glass.

Megan sat and watched as Andi started to seemingly empty the entire refrigerator of food. She didn't feel right not pitching in and the brief hug and kiss had left Megan distracted with arousal. Watching Andi move around the kitchen with that assured economy of movement she seemed to always have wasn't helping. Cook or kiss? She slid off the stool, went into the small kitchen, and looked over Andi's shoulder as she sliced the bread, waiting until she put the knife down to trace a kiss across the nape of her neck.

"You keep doing that and you're going to go hungry."

Megan traced a finger across Andi's ear, jingling the captive bead rings. "Maybe we need to work up an appetite," she whispered.

Andi leaned back, letting Megan run her hand through her short sandy blond hair and started to chuckle. "Really? Work up an appetite. Cheesy!"

Megan wrapped her arms around her from behind, pressing her body against her. "Hey, I'm new at this, give me a break."

Andi stretched her head back trying to reach Megan's lips, but they were too far apart to kiss and the attempt resulted in another bought of shared laughter.

"I have so much fun with you," Megan said, sliding her lips across Andi's neck.

"It's fun when I'm not terrified," Andi replied, reaching behind to put her hands on Megan's hips.

"Do I still scare you?" Megan whispered.

"Yes."

"But I'm a kind and gentle creature of the forest," Megan said, releasing her.

Andi turned and gave her a quick peck, then returned to cooking, breaking eggs into a bowl and adding milk and a dash of orange liqueur. "That's the secret to French toast. Booze. It makes everything better."

"Ooh, drunken adventures at 8:00am?" Megan commented, still hovering behind. As Andi started to whisk the mixture, Megan reached down and cupped her backside, sending batter across the counter.

"Stop that or I can't be held responsible."

"Stop what?" Megan said mischievously, kneading her ass through the tight jeans.

"One last chance."

Megan gave her bottom another caress and returned her lips to Andi's neck, tracing down her shoulder with tiny kisses.

Andi tried to beat the mixture for a few additional strokes before giving up any pretense, dropping the whisk, and spinning around. "Oh fuck this," she gasped out, capturing Megan's mouth in a desperate aggressive kiss. As the other woman's tongue darted between her lips to taste her, Megan found herself being walked backwards, Andi's hands firmly on her hips, until she was pinned against the refrigerator.

Giving in to arousal, Megan put her hands around Andi's neck, pulling her head closer, fingers roaming through the soft dirty-blond hair and tickling behind her ears. The feeling of Andi's body crushing against hers was overwhelming, robbing her of any reason or purpose other than to meld with her.

Their mouths separated, as Megan gasped for breath her hands roamed across Andi's shoulders, tracing the contours of her body through the shirt.

"Bed?" Andi gasped, her voice desperate with need.

Andi was taking her to bed? The thought was at once both terrifying and wonderful, but desire was the obvious victor. Between kisses, Megan nodded and mumbled assent.

Easing back, Andi kissed Megan again and pulled her by the hips, guiding her in giggling stumble steps all the way to the bedroom. "Hands up," she said, taking a step back. Megan complied and Andi whisked the shirt over her head as if she was a child. Andi's face was different, pure lust and desire, and all of it directed straight at Megan, sending a jolt of electricity down her spine.

Megan unsnapped the buttons on Andi's top while she kicked off her shoes and fumbled at her belt, unclasping it and skinning her jeans and panties off in a single motion. Letting her shirt fall off her arms, Andi knelt, brushing her lips across Megan's tummy as she slid the tan cargo pants down, following the dropping fabric with a line of kisses across her panties.

Megan shivered, feeling Andi's hot breath against her. She was beyond aroused, her pussy wet, nipples hard, and her clit throbbing almost to the point of pain. She put her hands on Andi's head, running fingers through her short hair and gasping as Andi kissed her sex, the tip of her nose nuzzling Megan through the sheer fabric.

"You smell so good," Andi traced kisses across her thighs.

Megan stepped backwards, pulling Andi with her, and let herself fall back onto the bed. Looking up at Andi, the reality washed over Megan that she was in bed with another woman. The fantasies she'd had as a teenager, long suppressed and mostly forgotten, suddenly becoming manifest. "Is this really happening?" she giggled.

"It's happening Meg," Andi tickled Megan's thigh, tracing her fingers across the bare skin.

Megan reached down and curled her legs up to slip out of her panties. Andi lay next to her and they kissed gently, Andi's hand caressing her naked hip. Megan looked into her beautiful blue eyes as Andi's hand slowly moved from the hipbone across to her sex. As she felt a fingertip tracing the sensitive skin between her leg and pelvis, Andi looked at her as if to question her advance. Megan nodded and spread her legs to give admission, holding her breath nervously.

Andi's touch was gentle, her hand softly palming Megan's sex. The warm touch was overwhelming and Megan mewled in response, the pressure against her clit setting off rippling waves of pleasure up her body. She pressed herself forward, grinding against Andi's hand.

"You're so beautiful," Andi said, kissing her. "So soft."

"Thank you," was all Megan could think of to say.

"For what?" Andi smiled, tracing a finger across the velvety folds

"For being so gentle and so... Oh Andi" she gasped, as she felt a finger slide between the ripples of flesh and brush softly against her clit.

"So wet for me," Andi said, her finger making languid strokes against the hard sensitive nub.

Andi's hand withdrew and she began to slowly work her way down Megan's body, covering every warm inch with her lips. Kisses across her neck, kisses across her breasts, a brief tug of lips on her pebbled nipple, then a tongue circling it and tracing lower. Tracing across her stomach. Across her hip. Another staccato line of kisses and hot breath against her sex. Megan legs spread wide as eager fingers moved her folds aside and an incredible pleasure radiated out as Andi's tongue lashed her clit. The feeling sent her immediately over the edge, Megan's body arching off the bed, every muscle trembling as the sensuous ripples passed through her.

No sooner had her body come back to rest from the tremors of her orgasm than Andi began once again to pleasure her. Her tongue this time gentle, caressing every inch of Megan's sex as she lay back unable to do anything but clutch at the sheets. The feelings were incomprehensible. Every inch of her skin was alive. Even the soft touch of the sheets or a brief flutter of wind through the open window sending sparks through her. Finally, pleasure building, Andi returned to her clit, circling it gently and firmly until once again Megan broke apart under her.

"That was…" Megan's voice faded off as Andi pulled herself up and they looked into each other's faces.

Andi leaned forward and Megan met her mouth in a deep slow kiss. She grinned, embarrassed, as their lips broke.

"What?" Andi asked amused, tracing circles gently against Megan's chest.

"I can taste myself," Megan's face flushed red.

"It's a terribly wonderful taste," Andi whispered, her fingers gently brushing Megan's hair from her eyes and their lips meeting again.

Megan looked down and hesitated. "I… I'm not sure I know what to do," she admitted.

"You don't have to do anything if you don't want to," Andi said kindly as she stroked the soft skin of Megan's cheek.

"Oh, I want to," Megan almost laughed out loud. "I have wanted to forever, I just don't want to… Don't want to do a bad job for you."

"Touch me like you'd touch yourself," Andi said, her voice confident and kind. "Watch my face and you'll be able to tell if something feels good."

And so Megan did, reaching down, she caressed Andi's waist for a moment before slipping a finger into the warm wet crease. She smiled at Andi as she took a moment to explore her sex. Megan wasn't sure what she'd expected. Andi's body was both so like hers and not at the same time. She delved further, slipping a digit inside, delighted at the way Andi gasped and closed her eyes when she did.

"Is that good? I didn't know if you'd want…"

"You inside me? Yes."

Megan slid a second finger in and pressed down with her palm against Andi's clit, gently massaging her. "Good?" she asked.

"Wonderful baby," Andi purred.

Megan crept down in the bed and tentatively caressed the petite pink areola of Andi's breast with her tongue, glancing up to watch her face between each new motion. She circled the small stiff nipple before covering it with her lips. She gently suckled as Andi whimpered, her body trembling under Megan's attentions.

Oh my god, I'm kissing a girl's boobs. The thought that appeared out of nowhere and Megan almost broke into nervous giggles, but fought it back, gently spreading kisses across the pliant orbs.

Andi moaned with pleasure as Megan slid her fingers out of her and began to caress the tiny stiff bud of her clit. She took a fingertip and made little circles, pressing down firmly, just the way she did to herself. Still lavishing attention on Andi's breasts with her mouth, she couldn't quite see the other woman's face, but from the way Andi's fingers were digging into her back and the sexy writhing of her body, Megan guessed she was doing something right.

"Oh that, more of that," Andi gasped as Megan pressed her finger more firmly onto her clit and added a second finger to the rhythmic circling. Megan knew she was close and squizzled up on the bed, wanting to look into her eyes when she came. Andi took her breasts in short gasps, mouth opened, her eyes were full of wonder and adoration. Megan's heart leapt, delighted she could ever elicit that kind of reaction from another human being.

She leaned forward, capturing Andi's mouth. With her hand, she increased the speed at which she stroked her below. Andi was so close. Finally, she broke apart, her eyes closing, mouth silently gasping, and fingers digging into Megan's back. Megan tried to keep her on the edge as long as possible, drawing out her orgasm until, finally, Andi collapsed on the bed panting for breath.

Megan snuggled in, resting her head on the other woman's shoulder.

"Are you sure you've never done that before?" Andi teased.

"Very sure," Megan giggled nervously.

"Are you OK with it? With everything?" Andi asked, caressing Megan's cheek.

"There were a couple of times when I thought to myself 'am I really doing this,' but I'm very OK with it. That was. I've never come like that or enjoyed making someone else come as much. It was beautiful. You're beautiful."

"I feel the same way," Andi gently eased away and propped herself up and looked into Megan's eyes. "I think that extra feeling is what happens when you're in love with someone."

The words tore through Megan, the truth of the simple statement shocking her to the core. She looked up into Andi's eyes, that depth of blue, her smile, the angles of her face, and searched her feelings silently. The quiet went on for what seemed like forever and she thanked whatever powers there were that Andi gave her the time. Megan wanted to say it. She'd wanted to say it weeks ago on that night that turned so horrible. Was it safe to admit? To make it real by speaking it out loud?

Leaning forward for a kiss, Megan's voice was barely a whisper, "I think you're right because I am absolutely head over heels in love with you."

Epilogue

Labor Day Weekend

"That went well, I thought," Andi said, her voice completely serious as she pulled her Subaru into the driveway, gray gravel crunching under the tires.

"Compared to 9/11 or Pearl Harbor?" Megan laughed.

"Really Megan?" Andi said seriously, leaning across the car seat. "It wasn't that bad at all. Your mother was? Well I get what you say about her now. But the rest of the family is nice and your niece is unbelievably cool."

"Not niece. Cousin, once removed? I think? I don't really get all the cousins and nieces and stuff." The fifteen year old had clung to Megan and Andi like a life preserver from the minute they walked in, telling them about her plans to revive the GSA at her high school, and extracting a promise to take her to Provincetown.

"Going back to the less supportive relatives, you realize the tall guy you were talking baseball with was Josh right?"

"Well, his name was Josh, but I don't know what that means otherwise," Andi answered. "He seemed nice enough to me."

"That would be Josh, my cousin who snagged a bunch of beers when he was seventeen and shoved us in a closet because it was oh so hilarious?"

"Really? I wonder if he even remembers. Maybe we should thank him. Seven minutes in heaven turned out to be pretty good, even if the big payoff was fifteen years later," Andi said brushing the backs of her fingers against Megan's cheek.

"Sixteen years and you're right; he's never actually been that bad. He was just being a big lunkhead," Megan gave Andi a kiss and turned to get out of the car. "I'm afraid my mother will never approve of you, but don't take it too badly. She doesn't approve of me either. She doesn't even have the excuse of being homophobic. She would be if she thought about it, but you're not rich or powerful enough for her to even get around to the gay thing. You have to be a mover and shaker or a millionaire or something for her to approve."

"Yeah," Andi said, putting her arms around Megan. "A millionaire? Don't tell her how much the cottages are worth, I don't think I could take her approval," Andi tickled Megan's behind. "At least she didn't call me 'the lesbian' or 'Andi-the-man-dee' which puts her one up on the first time we met in May."

"You're never going to let me forget that are you?" Megan jabbed her in the shoulder.

"Never, ever, my love," Andi said, taking Megan's hand.

"You should have seen the puss she made when you gave her that bear hug. Would it be terrible for me to admit I almost laughed out loud?" Megan fumbled with the keys as Lola barked on the other side of the door. She opened it and the terrier bounded out, yipping happily and running little figure eights between their legs as they stepped into the house. Megan had only officially moved in a few weeks earlier, trying to clear the summerhouse for her family's annual Labor Day gathering, but for all intents and purposes, she'd been living in the cottage since June.

"You know," Andi said, her voice full of emotion, "I love watching you unlock the door because it reminds me it's *our* home now."

"Our home..." Megan echoed and stepped into the cottage.

Printed in Poland
by Amazon Fulfillment
Poland Sp. z o.o., Wrocław